A
GOOD
DAY
TO
DIE

A GOOD DAY TO DIE

J A M E S C O L T R A N E

W. W. Norton & Company   New York • London

For my children

For information about permission to reproduce selections from this
book, write to Permissions, W. W. Norton & Company, Inc., 500 Fifth
Avenue, New York, NY 10110

The text of this book is composed in Meno with the display set in
Trade Gothic Condensed
Composition by Gina Webster
Manufacturing by Courier Companies, Inc.
Book design by Dana Sloan

Library of Congress Cataloging-in-Publication Data

Coltrane, James.
    A good day to die / James Coltrane.
        p.   cm.
    ISBN: 978-0-393-33666-5
    I. Title.
PS3553.04775G66   1999
813'.54—dc21   98–46970
                                CIP

W. W. Norton & Company, Inc., 500 Fifth Avenue, New York, N.Y. 10110
http://www.wwnorton.com

W. W. Norton & Company Ltd., 10 Coptic Street, London WC1A 1PU

1 2 3 4 5 6 7 8 9 0

Only the prisoner can free the jailer.

        —José Martí

May you choke on the bones of your father.

        —Cuban Insult

A GOOD DAY TO DIE

CHAPTER 1

HE CROUCHED BEHIND the shattered sill of the window, his legs folded beneath him, the old man by his side. High overhead a quad-prop Tupolev slowed above the harbor. The hotel was old, built for tourists before the first revolution. A rocket had taken off a good part of the roof; behind them the hallway gave on space, a sheer drop through rooms comically cross-sectioned, furniture still in place, picture frames cocked sideways. Across the boulevard, the roofs of burned-out apartment houses lay dark; below, ancient Chevys and a few Russian coupes flitted between the dead stoplights. Far down the boulevard he saw the white high-rise and the forest of antennas, gray in the fading summer light.

"That's the station there?" Jorge Ortega asked.

"The tall one," old Felipe said.

"I don't remember it."

"It's new. The old one's further down, below the ballpark."

Jorge spread the acetate map on the carpet. It was only half accurate, taken from a recon plane a decade ago. Santa Rosa was a small city, obscure, on the far side of the island; Jorge supposed that was the reason the Company had picked it, and therefore him.

The old man looked over his shoulder, muttering. He was tall but solid, in a navy Detroit Tigers windbreaker and baggy jeans and scuffed workboots. In his face you could see he'd been a drinker but had come back from that. He wheezed from the climb up the fire escape and his cigarillos. He reminded Jorge of the professor in El Salvador, the slight stoop, the nonchalant acceptance of his duty. The professor, poor bastard. He did not want to think of El Salvador, especially now. It was only a year ago but it seemed another life. That was when he still believed in something. What? And why? There was no reason to.

He clamped the thought off, concentrated on the station, let his expensive Langley training kick in. Objective, strategy, tactic. Break it down, fit it together. First, they needed a way in.

"You can't see the entrance from here."

"Behind those trees," the old man said. "There's a marquee over the doors and a park across the street." It was an obscure peasant dialect, more formal, and Jorge had to pause and process it.

"I remember."

"There's a second entrance on the far side, and a freight elevator in back we can use for the retreat."

It was too early to think retreat, but even he began to picture the elevator. A mistake. First things first.

"Can we come back tonight for a better look?"

"It is done," Felipe said.

"The guards don't sleep in the building."

"They're stationed at the armory, under Lieutenant Clemente." The old man pointed, careful not to lean too close to the window. There were rumors the government had snipers positioned throughout the city.

Jorge took his night-vision glasses from the brushed-steel case and flicked them on. They hummed like a flash attachment and the outlines of the buildings shimmered a brilliant green. Castro had been dead nearly a year, and tattered black bunting still hung from every facade, even those halved and blasted away. The sea breeze gave the cloth a false motion Jorge could not afford to ignore. He adjusted the ridged wheel until bits of letters on the marquee showed through the waving trees. He thought he saw the toe of a boot, the striped leg of a dress uniform. He swung the glasses across the street and the world blurred, then snapped back again. The armory had concrete highway dividers drawn up in front of it, like the White House.

"There's no one in the guard booth."

"They're there," Felipe assured him. "Clemente's got them hidden."

"You sound afraid of him, *hombre.*"

"Don't make fun of me. I've seen the others and I've seen Clemente."

Jorge followed a gray Saracen down the boulevard, its turret swiveling. A woman on the sidewalk covered her face with her purse and ran for a doorway. "How many sleep in the armory?"

"Sixteen, not including the corporal. At night he goes home to his wife."

"The airfield barracks?"

"A hundred twenty-five, half of them professional."

"How many do we have?"

"Over a hundred, but we're in small bands and our weapons are garbage. How many will you need?"

"I'll tell you when I get a better look at the station. It's not getting in I'm worried about, it's getting back out."

"You really believe that will happen?"

Jorge Ortega surveyed the street, the armory. Far across the city rose the lights of the ballpark like giant flyswatters. In the distance, an ancient MiG screamed up from the airfield. "No," he said, "but it would be nice."

They climbed steadily up the mountainside, old Felipe in the lead with his walking stick. Palm fronds and the waxy leaves of banana trees nodded, but no breeze reached them. The jungle had the same feel as El Salvador—the humidity, the same stench of decay—and he didn't like it. He could take it though, as long as he didn't start seeing Catalina. As long as he didn't start remembering.

There was no trail that he could see. The straps of his pack cut into his shoulders; it was a rule that those coming up from the city should bring as much as they could. Along with Jorge's equipment,

Felipe's pack was stuffed with flour and cornmeal and several dozen boxes of shotgun shells. In his, Jorge had the PRC-60 radio; the plastique was hidden in a hollow battery pack.

They met a dribble of a rill and the old man led him up the bed, his boots splashing among the mossy rocks. The face of the mountain grew steeper until finally the stream stopped at the base of a sheer cliff, the water shattering on black rock, pricking his face. Felipe squeaked as he breathed, yet his face was the same, not at all red, and unlike Jorge he wasn't sweating. He sloughed off his pack and set it on a rock, cupped his hands and took a drink.

"Wait here," he said. "I'll give them the signal."

"How much further is it?" Jorge asked. He didn't like the idea of sitting defenseless in the middle of the jungle. He'd done that enough in Guatemala, Colombia, Nicaragua. He'd signed on after the Marines, hoping he would end up here, had kept his eye on Castro's fading health like a thief watching a house. But Castro hung on, and with every mission the job came to take on a sameness he hated, if only because it blunted his true ambition. Even the edge of danger no longer motivated him, only proved the people above him had underestimated his risk, left him to correct their paper mistakes with blood. Only minutes ago they'd passed the steaming droppings of some government cavalry. The Fidelistas recruited peasants who knew the hills from childhood; it didn't give Jorge confidence.

"Not far," Felipe said. "Rest. I won't betray you."

"I know, uncle."

He watched the old man disappear into the underbrush, the tangle of lianas. In all honesty he did not trust Felipe, for Jorge Ortega had learned even before leaving Miami for the war—even before Catalina and the professor—to trust no one. His father, a good cop, had taught him that. His mother had left early on, and when his father was satisfied that Jorge had become a man that would never forget that lesson, he locked the basement door and went down the stairs and sat in his BarcaLounger in front of *The Game of the Week* and fit the barrel of his service revolver into his mouth and blew the back of his head all over the striped wallpaper. So being alone did not bother Jorge; it was the idea that promises might actually be kept that worried him.

4

His promise to take the station was not his own. Forbes had assigned it to him, knowing Jorge's family had come from Santa Rosa, that he'd spent a sentimental winter here undercover as a minor-league scout, and that he had the requisite communications experience. He'd been a DJ in college, and that had clinched it for Forbes. They met alone in a hotel room above West Palm Beach, the waves breaking white in the distance. Forbes came in street clothes and smelled of cologne. In the Corps he was only a major, but since Peña's helicopter had been shot down he was the rebels' best general.

"Taking the station doesn't mean a thing," Forbes said, sweeping his hand over the whole valley. He only had three fingers, and his thumb was a nub, flat as an eraser. He'd been in everything since Korea. "Taking the station and being on air providing the latest, most correct information after the first wave is breaking even. It's the least we expect."

"Yessir," Jorge said, unsure what else he could do.

"All news all the time, that's what we're talking about. It's got to be fast and accurate. I need fifteen minutes of clear transmission." He checked Jorge's eyes. "How many minutes do I need?"

"Fifteen."

"Negative. Give me forty-five and I might get fifteen. Okay," he said, rapping the map. "You'll have to get through a few *guardia* but they're nowhere near first-line troops. Your contact is in touch with indigenous forces—the hills are literally crawling with them. Intel hasn't got dossiers on any of them, so use as few as possible. I want this small. I want this clean. My real people need to know what's going on in the first fifteen minutes or I'm not going to commit, it's that simple. We get the harbor, we're on—we pull everyone out of the woodwork. If we can't get landed, there's a real possibility for a slaughter, and you know everyone's going to say Bay of Pigs, and that'll be all she wrote, understand me?"

"Yes, sir."

"*You* are going to make sure that doesn't happen—*you*, not your people. You don't have people, you don't have anything. They say you like it that way, is that right?"

"Yes, sir."

"I like it that way too. Semper Fi doesn't always cut it." He rose and gave Jorge his hand; the missing fingers made it feel stiff, like a mannequin's. "You doing this for me or for your country?"

"My country," Jorge said.

"Which one is that?" the general asked. "Be careful how you answer."

"Both," he'd said, but now, waiting for Felipe, Jorge wondered if he belonged to either. He didn't trust Felipe *or* Forbes, yet here he was, a year after Castro, the state grave still heaped with flowers, the tribute of a grateful nation. Unavoidable, really, being here. Fate. He picked up a pebble and flipped it into the stream, then did it again, thinking.

From below came a high-pitched whinny. Jorge stayed his hand and faced the sound but there was nothing but green. For an instant he pictured himself killing the old man, his K-bar slipping through the tendons of his wattled neck, his dead weight in Jorge's arms. He remembered hauling the professor off the back of the pickup, the sound the escaping gas made, then shook his head to clear it.

He listened, and in a minute heard soft, professional steps—no swishing leaves, no clash and rattle of a rifle sling, just the considered pad of feet against earth. He drew his pistol and backed against the cliff. The steps were coming from his left, the path Felipe had taken, but there was more than one person. Jorge knelt and braced his elbow on his knee, leveling the weapon where a man's chest would appear. The footsteps were louder now, less thoughtful. The trigger bit into his finger, and then a single tan workboot cleared the rock face.

It was Felipe. Following him was another man, also—ridiculously—in a Tigers windbreaker, with an M-16 slung across his back; his nose was smeared across his face, and a scar disappeared into his beard. The two began to laugh at the pistol, but Jorge put a finger to his lips and tipped his head down the mountain.

In a single motion, the man with Felipe unslung the M-16 and hugged the ground. He had the barrel pointed at Jorge's face.

Behind him, Felipe shrugged helplessly.

"You are El Tiante?" the man hissed.

"I am," Jorge whispered.

"You have identification to prove this?" He pulled from his windbreaker half of a baseball card, the right side of Luis Tiant—except to

Jorge's surprise the great pitcher was a Cleveland Indian and not the Red Sock on Jorge's matching half. Was it a bluff, a setup?

Jorge dug in his jeans and offered him the card.

As the man lowered his rifle to take it, Jorge ripped the weapon from his hands and turned it against him.

The man ignored him, more interested in the cards. They fit together perfectly; the Cleveland Tiant looked backward while his Red Sock body rotated toward home plate. "You're him," the man said grudgingly.

"You have identification for me?" Jorge challenged him.

The man tossed the cards in his face and got up and walked away. Jorge jerked the bolt back, but the weapon was empty. The man vanished up the path. "*Culo,*" Jorge swore.

Felipe tipped his head for Jorge to follow, then set off. Jorge hefted his pack and hustled to catch up. The other was far ahead, just a shape moving through the lush jungle.

"What's your friend's name?" Jorge asked.

"He's not my friend. He's Aurelio, the section commander. He's afraid you'll take his best men from him and waste them on this one mission. He wasn't always such a rabbit. You're not our first *americano*, or didn't the *generalissimo* tell you?"

"How many have there been?"

"You're the third since Fidel."

"Should I ask what happened to them?"

"They were *blancos*, not one of the people."

"Does that matter?" Jorge asked.

"Who *you* are matters. Forbes told me. I knew your grandfather. He was my *generalissimo* when we first fought the Fidelistas. I was there at Mariel, working the guns for him."

"You're too young for Mariel."

"That morning I was a boy, and that evening I was an old man."

"You have my respect, Don Felipe."

"He said you were in the desert war."

"It was over in a month," Jorge said. "We had to take pills in case of a gas attack. Nerve agents. The enemy was in bunkers. First our planes bombed them with napalm, then the engineers bulldozed what remained, then we came in behind our armor."

"So you've learned respect."

"No," Jorge said, "I learned not to look."

"That's respect, no?"

"I suppose. And Aurelio, has he learned this?"

"He's learned not to trust *americanos*. He doesn't like to lose men."

"Who does?" Jorge said.

The old man stopped and Jorge had to. Around them the jungle was quiet. Felipe looked him in the eyes. Yes, Jorge thought, the professor, a true believer. When had he lost that? He was like a fighter who had given up but still heard the bell, wandered out splay-footed to meet his punishment.

"Sometimes it's a necessity. Your grandfather knew that." Felipe kept looking at him, as if letting it sink in, then turned and planted his walking stick and trudged up the mountain.

Aurelio was waiting for them in a clearing, Felipe's pack at his feet. He was drinking from a canteen. He held it out to Felipe. "El Tiante," he said, "I'll take my rifle."

Jorge unslung it. He wanted to throw it at the man, but he knew he'd have to work with him. He handed it to him, careful of the barrel.

Aurelio pulled up one sleeve of his windbreaker. On his arm, beneath the skin, a set of green numbers bled into each other—a prison tattoo from the *federale*. "Here's your identification. Now why have you come to my section?"

"A small operation, which is my business."

"If it's in Santa Rosa, it's my business."

"I didn't say it was in Santa Rosa."

Felipe wiped his lips with the back of his arm and handed the canteen to Jorge. Aurelio looked to the old man, but he said nothing.

Aurelio stood. "We haven't been here three years by pissing in our own well. We operate beyond the mountains, in the hills around Arriaga. You can't live and operate in the same place. It's fine for Americans who can fly to Miami and live in apartment buildings, but not for us. This is our home. I've got to make sure we'll still have an operation when you're gone."

"I understand." He handed the canteen back, and Aurelio capped it.

"I don't think you do, but it's not my place to say. Forbes says we'll assist you, we'll assist you." He patted Felipe's pack. "You're a radioman, no? You're interested in the station, possibly to coordinate a landing."

Jorge could feel his eyes narrowing, a scowl crossing his mouth.

"My young Tiante, a revolution is either all secrets or none. None is sometimes better." He shouldered the old man's pack. "Here, I'll show you *our* secret. It may save us both some trouble."

He led them over a bald rock ledge speckled with moss and into a dusty gully. It was quiet here, insects tangling in front of their faces, birds sailing from limb to limb. Far off, Jorge could hear the thrum of a big prop plane, a newer Tupolev from the sound of it. The Company flew Spookys—C-47s with electric miniguns mounted at the waist ports; their old Allisons made a higher, whinier buzz. They also ran decommissioned Cobras and Hueys out of the DEA field on Key Largo, a completely black operation. Supposedly one would come on Monday to pick him up at the ballpark, landing in straight center field. Though it was only three days away, Jorge couldn't picture it. Strangely, it didn't trouble him.

The path dead-ended in a wall of bougainvillea. Aurelio lifted it aside like a curtain to reveal a crooked hole. They had to take their packs off to fit through.

Aurelio had a red-lens flashlight. The cavern was cool inside, the floor a fine dust. Jorge ducked and laid a hand on Felipe's back.

"Be careful here." Aurelio shone the light on three small rocks.

"It's mined," Felipe said.

They turned a corner, and Aurelio stopped in front of an olive drab canvas thrown over two coffin-sized lumps. With one arm he drew it aside, and there in the glow of the flashlight sat two old PRC-25s still in their crates, the excelsior nestlike. In training, Jorge had seen films of them in Vietnam. Even their shorter antennas were an easy target; the narrator praised their durability, then called them obsolete.

"Do they work?"

Aurelio unhooked the headset and clicked a switch and the receiver filled with static. He seemed pleased.

"You should disconnect the battery packs when you're not using them," Jorge said.

"The other one is," Aurelio said. "I hooked this one up just for you."

"You have the long antennas?"

"Long *and* short. And look at these." He shone the light to one side, revealing a pair of Russian walkie-talkies from the late eighties. Jorge knew their range was too limited to be any real help, but picked one up to admire it.

"We killed a pair of *guardia*," Aurelio said.

"Congratulations."

"They stopped one of our trucks on the road between Segovia and Maria del Rey. It was a shipment of mortars. We had two men in the back."

"Have you killed many of Clemente's men?" Jorge asked.

"Oh no," Felipe said, "these weren't Clemente's."

"No," Aurelio said. "We've found it best to leave him alone."

"What about the airfield?"

"There isn't much we can do without help."

"You can't drop a mortar on the runway?"

Neither man answered, and Jorge thought it better not to press. It was already starting badly. He could rely somewhat on the old man, but the commander obviously preferred his own security to even the least risky of missions. In the Corps they had a name for such officers—the walking dead. But maybe he was right. If Forbes didn't commit, it was a wash, any responsibility denied, the hardware buried, America's hands clean. There were any number of front groups in Miami poised to take the blame, the only consequence an instant visibility, a sudden windfall of contributions.

Aurelio pointed hopefully to the radios. "With these you can reach your people offshore."

"We still need the transmitter," Jorge said, though what the commander said was true.

"*Ay*, you're determined to bring Clemente here." He looked at the radios gloomily, then flung the tarp back over them. "When it's just horses, that's fine, but if Clemente sends his helicopters we're finished here, and where can we go? Tell me that, Tiante."

"You sound like a bureaucrat," Felipe said with distaste. "Worrying about your house."

The vehemence with which the old man spoke surprised Jorge, but Aurelio only shrugged.

"These aren't the only mountains," Jorge said.

"What do you know of mountains?" Aurelio said, his voice filling the cave. "What right do you have, an American, telling us what to do?"

"There are others, if you're afraid."

"We're not afraid," Felipe assured him. "It's just been a hard summer."

"It's not the summer," Aurelio said. "It's the war. It's been going on too long."

"A year," the old man said, "the true war. Not even. You're just no good at losing. Why fight if you're afraid to lose? I don't understand. You weren't always like this, my friend."

"We're wasting time," Jorge said, to stop their philosophizing. They both looked at him strangely, and he was sorry he'd said it. "I still need to go back after dark and take a closer look."

"He's right," Felipe said. "We all know what we have to do."

"It's not what," Aurelio said, "it's how and when and where, and most important of all, why."

"And whom," Felipe said.

"Yes," Aurelio said, "but don't ask me that yet. I haven't decided what we're doing." He turned as if it were a final statement, taking the light with him, and Jorge had to grope in the dark for the slippery nylon of the old man's windbreaker. As they shuffled through the dark, his feet stumbled over rocks, sank into soft spots. Felipe squeaked as he breathed. It was ridiculous, Jorge thought; here he was, in a country he loved yet which would never accept him, following an old drunk and a coward in the dark. For the first time since he'd dragged his pack ashore this morning, he laughed.

"What's so funny?" Aurelio asked.

"Nothing," Jorge said. "Nothing at all."

AFTER A SECOND break for water, they came out of the jungle onto a broad path. It was shaded and muddy in the center, a few hoofprints visible.

"Cavalry?" Jorge asked. He leaned over to count the holes in the shoes.

"Maybe ours," Aurelio said. "How a horse is shod is no guarantee. It's a game we play." As he spoke he kept glancing up and down the trail, inching toward the cover of the jungle, and Jorge thought it best not to panic him by investigating.

They followed a game trail, Felipe walking drag, covering their backs. Though Jorge was in the middle, Aurelio was a good head shorter, and a spiderweb broke over Jorge's face. The palmettos stabbed at his hands.

They stopped again, and Felipe cut a Milky Way bar into three pieces. Jorge gobbled his and found Aurelio staring at him.

"You haven't eaten," Aurelio noted. "At camp you'll have supper with us."

Farther along, the mountain was loud with frothing streams. They followed the narrow bottom of a ravine, the ferns slashing at their knees, until they came upon a calm pool beside a rock wall. The water dribbled over a stone dam. Above them rose a series of ledges like steps which suddenly cut away so they couldn't tell if someone was looking down on them. The whole formation was topped by triple canopy, the light beneath dusky and green and smelling of fungus. It would be invisible from the air, a perfect place to camp, and as they slogged through the pool, Jorge saw a man in camo utilities sitting on one of the lower ledges with an M-16 across his knees. He glanced up from a beer can he was piercing with a bayonet. He had muttonchop sideburns that connected with his mustache, like a picture of Clapton from the sixties.

"*Hola,*" he said. "Who's with you?"

"Felipe and a radioman," Aurelio said, and climbed the natural stairs out of the water. Above yawned the mouth of a cave, a line of clothes drying in the filtered sunlight. The smell of frying onions drifted down, and now Jorge really was hungry.

"Radioman. Come for the station, eh?" The soldier shook his head and pointed the bayonet at Jorge's pack. The muttonchops were comic, almost false-looking, like a cheap disguise, a dimestore revolutionary. "Plastique in the battery case?"

Jorge didn't answer, and the man laughed and winked at him. "Leave your pack outside the cave, dead man. There's a fire in there."

"Plastique needs a fuse," Aurelio said.

"*Stupido,* all plastique needs is a flame. The *americano* leaves the pack outside."

"Rafael," Felipe said, offended, "he's the grandson of the great Ortega."

"The great Ortega," the man in utilities said, impressed, rising to take Jorge's hand. "That's different. He may blow us all up then."

"I'll leave the battery outside," Jorge agreed.

"Don't," Aurelio said. "He's a gypsy, he talks nonsense."

"*De nada,*" Jorge said. It is nothing. He shrugged off his pack. While he dug through it, Aurelio said he'd check on the food and went into the cave. The old man opened his pack and palmed the boxes of shells.

"Ah," Rafael said, "lovely," and took one for himself. The old man stole it back, and again Rafael winked at Jorge. He hacked at the top of the beer can with his bayonet, then twisted it off and frisbeed it into the pool.

"What are you making?" Jorge asked.

"Booby trap. You take a grenade, pull the pin and fit it in the can so it holds the spoon down. Then you tie the can to a branch. You tie the fishing line around the grenade and string it across the trail. The cavalry come along and poof—you're eating horsemeat instead of tortillas three times a day."

"To kill a horse is dishonorable," Felipe said.

"To let the communists take your country and make slaves of your children, that is dishonorable."

Jorge dug a carton of Marlboros from his pack. Immediately, Rafael grabbed it. Jorge snatched it away, broke open one end and threw him a hardpack.

"Thank you, Ortega." He was oddly formal now, repentant, truly grateful.

Jorge offered Felipe a pack, which the old man accepted with a bow.

The two men lit up.

"You don't smoke?" Rafael asked.

"Bad for the wind," Jorge said.

"Good for the nerves," Felipe said.

"Our last *americano* didn't smoke either," Rafael said. "It must be an American thing. It's a shame, with such beautiful cigarettes."

"What was the last one's name?" Jorge asked.

"It was a funny name," Rafael said. "Ox."

"Oaks," Felipe said. "He was heavy, strong as a bear."

"Miguelito Oaks?"

"Yes," Rafael said. "He called himself Michael."

Jorge had never met the man, but his name was well known around the Company. He'd been in and out of Indonesia, Lebanon, Costa Rica—the usual hot spots. It was a surprise they'd sent someone so well known. Oaks seemed like one of those guys who couldn't die.

"What happened to him?"

"The worst that can happen. He was captured. It was only a few weeks ago—" He stopped, and Jorge looked where he was looking.

14

Above them, Aurelio had come out of the cave and was sniffing the air. "Marlboros?"

Jorge waved him over.

"The food's almost done," Aurelio said.

They all sat on the ledge above the pool, smoking.

"So," Jorge said, "what happened to Oaks?"

Rafael said nothing.

"He was stupid," Aurelio said. "He went into the city with Luz to do reconnaissance and the police picked him up because he was a *blanco*. Very stupid. He wouldn't trust us, he had to do it himself."

"Paranoid," Felipe said.

"It's understandable," Jorge said.

"He hung himself in his cell," Aurelio said, "if you believe *La Figueroa*. Your country's trying to get his body back. We're hoping it will be a great scandal."

"And if that happens to me?"

"Let's hope it doesn't."

From above came a clatter of pots and pans.

"Go help the women," Aurelio told Felipe, and the old man climbed the stairs, followed by Rafael with his M-16. Jorge made to get up, but Aurelio stopped him. He leaned over close to him. "Right now you trust the old man and not me," he whispered. "That will change."

Why, Jorge wanted to ask, but said nothing, merely shrugged off his arm and climbed the steps.

A black-haired girl in a peasant dress stooped as she came out of the cave mouth, carrying a pair of tin plates. As she straightened up, Jorge saw the blatant break of her nose, the raccoonlike bruises around the eyes. She had big features, strange and inescapable as a model's. She would have been pretty, he thought, and then she smiled, showing a missing bridge—a single canine left on the top right side, a double gap in the front like a hockey player. In the back of the pickup, Catalina's face had been swollen, her jaw sitting oddly off to one side; he knew he shouldn't look but couldn't stop himself. This wasn't his work, was it?

"*Hola*, comrade," the girl said, and Jorge said, "*Salud*," and was careful not to stare or look away. She set the sectioned tin plate in front of him, and he noticed she had the same tattoo on her arm as

Aurelio, the green numbers under the skin, except hers weren't smudged by time, they were crisp, newly minted. Even with teeth, with her nose healed, she would be nowhere near as pretty as Catalina, would be an insult to her memory, a trifling second best.

Supper was tortillas and beans and rice with a blazing salsa over everything. The girl crossed her ankles and sat down beside him with the other plate and dug in with her fork. She caught him looking and smiled at him again, and he thought that he'd been wrong: she had once been stunning. How easy it was to crush someone, to take away everything. His father had only known the wrong side of that equation, his mother leaving him empty, the days passing in a blur of work and TV dinners, ball games on the radio.

"You think I need dentures?" the girl said. "Watch me eat."

"I didn't mean to stare."

"It's all right, I do it too. Luz has a mirror. Sometimes I take it out and look at what they've done. It makes me feel good about killing them." He noticed she tried to speak without moving her lips; it was only when she smiled that she revealed the black gaps. He wondered if it was simple pity that made him think of loving her, this woman he had just met. He had not thought of anyone this way since Catalina. Perhaps that was all that was left for him—pity, the reflex to protect the innocent, the helpless. It wasn't love. He didn't know what it was, but like his other inabilities—to forget, to forgive—it cut at him.

He tried to eat slowly, but he'd had nothing but the piece of Felipe's Milky Way since coming ashore. He'd been in the Zodiac a good two hours fighting the chop, and he needed to sleep. A bottle of rum made its way around the circle. He wanted to pass but it was expected, so he took a hot, strong swig and sent it on.

"I'm lying," the girl said, and in the first rush of the rum she seemed striking to Jorge—yes, a woman he would notice on the street, in a crowded bus. "About the killing. I don't really feel good about it. It feels good to do it, and then that fades away and you have something else. You know what I am saying?"

"Yes," Jorge said, for an instant flashing back to El Salvador, the power lines swooping across the valley, Catalina on her burro. Across the circle, Rafael was watching him, grinning. Jorge wiped the last of the sauce up with his tortilla.

"My name is Gloria," she said, and waited for Jorge to introduce himself. It was formal, like courtship, and he had the idea the others were watching them.

"Aurelio says you're here for the station."

"It was a secret once."

Aurelio laughed. "Look out for a man who believes in secrets!"

"Gloria," Rafael said, "tell him how you lost your teeth with Señor Donaldson."

"This was the first one?" Jorge asked.

"Yes," Gloria said. "Tomaso, we called him. *Pobre* Tomaso. He wasn't a fool like Señor Oaks. He saved my life."

"Perhaps," Felipe agreed.

"Be silent, uncle," Gloria said. "It's *my* story."

The rum came around as she was telling it. The two of them had been in a jeep coming up the mountain one night when they turned a corner and ran into a cavalry patrol. Donaldson never slowed down. "If he'd hesitated an instant," she said, "we would have been killed." The communists opened up, their muzzles flashing in the dark, and the horses parted. They flew down the narrow road, branches reaching in, tearing at her hair. She could hear gunfire behind them and the trampling of hooves. "And then," she said, "we're off the road and into the tree. Bang—that fast. The windshield"—she made a wall with her hand and slapped her forehead—"gets me like this, but I'm still awake. Señor Donaldson is lying between the seats like he's knocked out, but I can see he's shot, there are parts of his head missing. I can hear the horses coming for me and I run through the jungle holding my face so I don't cry out."

"Now comes my part of the story," Felipe said. Gloria leaned back and took the rum, gave way to the old man. "I'm the first to see her. I have no idea what's happening, and she comes up bleeding, holding her face. I have her lie down, and she holds out her hand, she has something in them for me. You know what it is, Ortega?"

"No," Jorge said.

"Her teeth, covered with blood. She wants me to fix them."

"It was shock," Gloria said. "Still, I'd like to have them back someday. Perhaps when we've won I'll have dentures put in—big shiny ones. Then when you look at me your heart will flutter like a boy's."

She was looking at Jorge knowingly, mockingly, but he knew they weren't idle words. He didn't know how to respond. Company protocol was clear—bring cigarettes, leave the women alone and don't take any money—but no one ever followed it. He wondered about Donaldson.

"My heart already does," Rafael said.

"Naturally," Gloria said. "Because you're a boy."

"All right, let's clean up," Aurelio told her, corking the rum. "You're embarrassing our guest."

"That is entirely my intention." She stacked Jorge's plate atop hers and rose and followed Aurelio into the cave, giving Jorge a gapped smile over her shoulder.

"She's a funny one," Jorge said.

"You think so?" Rafael said and winked at him.

"Why do you keep winking at me?"

"Because I'm jealous. I want you, but you want Gloria." He made kissing sounds, his lips pursed like a fish's.

"She's lost a great deal," Felipe said. "But she has a true heart. In a fight I'd choose her over anyone but Luz."

"Even me?" Rafael said, pretending to be crushed.

"You're a gypsy, you fight with your wits and your feet. A woman fights with everything." He made a fist and thumped his chest. "I'd take Luz over all of you, even the Ortega, if you'll excuse me."

Jorge nodded. "Who is Luz?"

"She cooked your supper. She's Aurelio's woman."

"Wrong," Rafael said. "Aurelio is Luz's man."

"He's even less than that now," said Felipe. "He let Oaks go into the city when he could have easily done it himself. He's been running scared since Donaldson was killed."

Jorge thought of what Aurelio had said about trusting the old man. It was fine, trust was a luxury. He'd stay out of their business, it was easier that way. That was the problem in El Salvador, getting to know them, eating with their families, listening to their politics, their faith in the church. It made it hard to turn away, to get done what was necessary. The professor had warned him, jokingly, but it was true. Ah, professor, he thought, what would you do now?

"You think Gloria's a mess," Rafael said, "wait till you see Luz. And with her it's natural."

"She's not blessed," Felipe agreed, "but she's the true *comandante* here. She's the only one left. Gloria's too willful to be a leader, I'm an old man, he fights when it pleases him, and Aurelio has lost heart."

"That can't be all of you," Jorge said.

"Two or three more, but they're farmers and it's the season. You're the third to come to us. Once we were twenty-five."

"I shouldn't need more than twelve."

"Tonight we're seven. Hector's standing guard above and César's on the main trail. Don't worry, El Marichal will have men."

"You won't get them to help you," Rafael said. "They know about the first two."

"Shut up," a tall woman said from the cave mouth. Her black hair was streaked with white; it fell to her waist and for an instant made her look younger. She wore utilities like Rafael, with a sheath on her belt and a pistol at her hip. She had the rum and a plate of supper. She sat down beside Jorge. Rafael hadn't lied—she was as ugly and old as Aurelio—but she carried herself with a regal manner, a deliberateness that wasn't affected. "El Marichal remembers the substation. He'll give us whatever we need."

She introduced herself, crushing Jorge's fingers like a trucker.

"You, gypsy," she said, "who's on guard below?"

Rafael popped up and scuttled down the stairs, flipping the ember of his cigarette into the pool. The day had given way to the lingering dusk of summer, and the jungle was alive with insects. Luz picked at her food; her hands were large, the knuckles knobby with work.

"You're from Forbes?" she asked nonchalantly, between bites of sopping tortilla. Her look told him he didn't have to answer, that she already knew. "I'm sure they told you what happened to the others. They can't keep their mouths shut. Remember that." She turned to Felipe. "Go help the girl, I need to talk with the Tiante."

The old man nodded and tottered off. Without his pack, he seemed frail. It pleased Jorge to see how well he hid his strength; it would be useful in the city.

"They say you're the son of the son of Ortega. Is this true?"

"Yes."

"You'll bring luck. We won't lack for men."

"I don't need many. I need this to be quiet."

"We agree then."

"What happened with Oaks? I'd always heard he was a good man."

"I'm not sure. I think the *guardia* knew he was coming."

"They didn't take you."

"It was fiesta. We were separated. I saw him go into the hotel with two men in white suits. That's the last I saw of him." She squeegeed the plate clean with her tortilla. "It wasn't me, and I'd know if it was Aurelio."

"I wasn't thinking that," Jorge said.

"The rest of them are. I understand he's not what he once was, but he's still for the cause. He's just cautious now."

"So am I."

"Rightfully," she said. "One other thing I should warn you about. Gloria. I know you'll try to make her feel beautiful, because that's the way in America, but don't ask for her heart."

"I wasn't planning on it," Jorge said.

"A man doesn't need plans to ruin things," Luz said. "She's stronger than you think. She has a great anger. She'll need you for a time and then she won't need you. That's how you should be."

"I only just met her."

"Aurelio told me how you looked at her, with the heart in the eyes. He's not stupid that way. She'll win you, you'll have her—the details don't interest me. Just remember, I need her after you leave."

"I'll remember."

"Aurelio says you're going into the city tonight."

"Very quickly," Jorge said. "I need to see the streets around the station. I've got to figure out how to get in."

"Take the old man. In the dark he's better than any of the young ones."

Luz looked into her plate as if she could read something there. She turned to Jorge but hesitated, her eyes unsure yet hopeful, questioning him. "So you think they'll actually try to land?"

"I can't worry about that. My job—"

"Yes, yes, but there's a real possibility? It's not just a bluff, a trick to cover something else?"

"I don't know," Jorge said, and he was being honest. Until now, he hadn't even entertained the question.

THE STREETCARS didn't work because of a rocket attack on the substation, so they had to take one of the ancient buses into the city. The storefronts were black, the glass reflective. Only a few streetlights burned weakly, blinking, fed by emergency current.

The bus was stifling. Jorge tried not to speak, afraid his accent might give him away. Felipe had traded him his windbreaker, which stank sharply of some muscle balm. The old man had changed into a short-sleeved shirt and slicked his hair back like the men who played chess in the park across from Jorge's apartment well into the night. He was pretending to read *La Figueroa,* leaning in close for the baseball scores, squinting, his lips moving. Now he reminded Jorge not of the professor but of his own father, home from work, kicking back in the BarcaLounger downstairs, slurping the foam from a newly cracked can of Bud. That same tired look around the eyes, the same rocklike stillness, as if they could stop time from flying past them. Old men all come to look the same, converge on the same exhausted point, become brothers. It wasn't something he'd have to worry about. They sat near the middle doors, behind a pair of women talking about the water problems, the rising prices. The road to Segovia was mined; in the markets there was no milk, no palm oil. The bus was full, the aisles packed.

"It's Friday night," Felipe explained, and Jorge thought he needed to be sharper; he had no idea what day it was, the date, anything. This morning he'd eaten steak and eggs on the fake fishing charter, stood in the tuna tower forking the rich, runny yolk up; then he hopped in the Zodiac, his clothes professionally weathered, blanched as if he'd failed to escape, the current ironically pushing him back to shore. He had barely seventy-two hours to get everything done. The fact that he was sitting made him feel he was wasting time. Offshore, Forbes's troops were cleaning the breeches of their weapons, filling their magazines— if they did in fact exist. And even if they did, they could disappear with the flick of a policy decision, a line crossed out of a speech, disowned, suddenly orphaned again. The revolution would go on slowly. Castro was dead and America didn't care.

Ah, but if they won . . .

Though it was fully night now, several people around them were wearing dark glasses, and Jorge wished he had some. Outside, the *guardia* strolled the streets in pairs, neat as plebes, their rifles slung. They shone their flashlights over pedestrians, tipping their caps to girls in halter tops and minis, dressed for the discotheques. He thought of Gloria, how she had run through the jungle clutching her bloody teeth. It didn't seem fair—and then he could not stop himself from seeing Catalina in the back of the truck with the others, her dirty feet bouncing against the lowered tailgate, the professor with his spectacles still hooked to one ear, the leather elbow patches of his tweed jacket wired together behind his back. Jorge had never thought it would go this far, and for days lay up in his hotel room, in shock, trying to convince himself it was not his fault. He had to make a coherent report and fax it to Langley, and then when he got back they no longer existed, had never been shot. The debriefing was short and clean. He had never been to El Salvador. Why go? they said. The fighting was over years ago. There was nothing there.

Here, there—he thought now that it was the same, the only difference was the politics. Well, that was everything, wasn't it?

Yes, but they'd taken her country too, just as Castro had hijacked his.

He would not debate the merits of socialism with a dead woman, not over the body of his grandfather, of his father, killed just as surely by the first revolution. He had long been without politics, that fanatic, blood-deep will to drive the communists from the entire continent broken down mission by mission, ground down to dust by each less-than-clean assignment, blown away by the intricate ironies of power and powerlessness. But this was different. Here his heart refused to hedge. Cuba would be free. Of this and nothing else he was certain.

"The next stop's ours," Felipe said, motioning for Jorge to pull the cord.

The bus lurched to a halt, and they fought their way through the crush of bodies and out onto the cool boulevard. Though they were several blocks away from the station, the *guardia* were everywhere. Their boots were new and they had Chinese AKs; it was a bad sign. Jorge had not brought a weapon in case they were stopped and patted down, but now he remembered Oaks and wished he had his pistol.

"Diego," Felipe said, and it took a minute for Jorge to respond. It was the name on the fake papers the Company made for him. Diego Vargas. It was as close to John Doe as they could get.

"What is it, *viejo?*" Jorge said.

"Just checking."

"There's no need."

It was foolish, an operation in the heart of the city. As they passed the teeming discos and open-air *mercado* with its torch-lit pyramids of oranges and lemons, its baskets of squid and peppers, he imagined the difficulty of a retreat. The ballpark was too far. Monday morning, the streets crowded with delivery trucks, dying Fiats, unmuffled scooters. Would Forbes bombard them from offshore or send in the F-111s? Would it be Apaches or the old Cobras, and how many civilians were they willing to kill?

In El Salvador the professor called it first a moral and then a political consideration, and Jorge had respected him for it. But the movement had to lose (they'd lost long ago, really, were only a remnant of the FMLN). There were moments when he imagined turning, actually becoming one of them, giving up the mission—going native, they said at the Company—but in the end he had done what he was sent to do, though now he thought that it had killed him as sure as it had Catalina. It was the first rule of the Company: always remember which side you're on.

No one's.

There was no time to think like this. It was the city that did it—the rotting smell of sewage stalled underground, of brick dust kicked up by rocket fire. It was strange how ruin prompted a sweet nostalgia in him. Kuwait, Managua, Ho Chi Minh City. He had grown to love these ugly capitals. It was a failure of the heart, he knew, but, ruined himself, he could not stop it. He wondered if his father had been like this before the end, if all Miami looked like it was falling down around him, going bad under the skin.

As they turned the corner below the decapitated hotel, Felipe nudged him in the ribs and tipped his head. "See who's in our room? Don't look."

"Who?"

"Sniper."

"It's all right," Jorge said. "We didn't leave anything."

"That's not the point. It's Clemente—he's ready for us."

Jorge stopped and turned to the old man, who looked at him, incredulous. Over his shoulder, Jorge could see down the street. Felipe was right, there was someone up there. Probably had them on a starlight scope right now.

"What are you doing?" Felipe asked.

"You're so terrified of Clemente, you should turn yourself in. He's a lieutenant, he's nothing."

"I'm just telling you things have changed."

"Keep talking," Jorge said. "Make it look like we're arguing." He cuffed the old man's shoulder, scanning the windows above.

"That won't be hard." Felipe struck him back. "I'm not like some who refuse to leave the safety of their cave, who live for their rum and their precious radios. I'm here with you in Clemente's city."

"It's not Clemente's city, it's ours." Jorge could make out three other gunmen above them, ranging all the way to the corner, one only a few stories up. The entire block was covered, their fields of fire generously overlapping. It would be like this throughout the city. They'd have communications. It would make it impossible to do things on foot, or even horseback, which he'd been saving as a last resort. Scooters wouldn't do it. They would need a car—two, possibly three.

"*Our* city?" the old man said. "Your eyes tell me different, *mi amigo.*"

"It's only a few men."

"It's the thought behind the men," Felipe said, pointing to his temple. "He's a thinker, Clemente. The others were wishful. Clemente has no wishes, only thoughts."

Jorge patted him on the arm, as if to forgive him. "Then we'll have to be thoughtful too."

"Agreed," the old man said, and they turned and continued down the street. It had been an unnecessary test, Jorge thought, though he was pleased the old man had passed so easily. He would have to keep an eye on Aurelio, despite Luz's assurances. It was tiring; the job would be hard enough.

Still, it was good to be working on it. It took his mind off his life—the empty apartment, the key left with his super to feed the angelfish. The vistas of intersections spawned possibilities, the alleys that connected secretly behind buildings, the underground parking garages that might provide the one needed link to the ballpark, Forbes's promised helicopter. He kept a map in his head, filling in details—bus stops and drink kiosks, manhole covers. Back at the cave he'd lay the retreat out on his acetate map with a magic marker, double-checking things with Felipe. It would give them hope, even if they didn't believe.

"There's another above the fish market there," the old man said. "You can see the end of his cigarette."

"I see him," Jorge said harshly, then apologized. He spoke softly then, still wary of his accent. "If they're in one place, they'll be in another. I'm not surprised."

"They will make it difficult."

"It's not supposed to be easy."

"I don't think the one who stays in the cave will like it."

"And you?" Jorge asked.

"I don't have to like it," Felipe said. "I just have to do it. But you may have trouble with the gypsy and the others."

"And El Marichal?"

"He's always been a good friend."

"It's not as if there's a choice."

"No," Felipe agreed, as if further discussion were pointless.

They turned onto a darkened street lined with shattered plate glass, nude mannequins strewn in pieces through the display windows. Across from the department store stood a stone archway framing blackness.

"Come," the old man said. "I'll take you through the park. That way we may sit as if we are visiting and take our time."

"Visiting."

"Like lovers, I mean to say. It's a common thing in the park. The *guardia* aren't a problem. In fact I've seen them here—heard them even."

"You come often?" Jorge joked.

"Do not make fun, my friend. Love is a gift whatever package it comes in."

The path curved through palm trees, groves of hibiscus. Broken glass scratched and tinkled under his feet. He heard a rustle off the walk, then a low groan—a raspy male voice pretending to be a woman's but not quite succeeding.

"Plus," the old man said, giving him a nudge, "sometimes the packages here are a surprise, uh?"

The first two spots they tried were occupied. The third was a low stone bench in a corner, still warm from the last couple, the smell of love still in the air. From here they could see across the street.

The first floor was a theater, and there must have been a promotion, because a crowd surrounded the doors beneath the darkened marquee. Merengue trilled from hidden speakers, the crowd dipping with the beat. There were eight doors, Jorge noted—four pairs, deeply tinted glass in chrome frames. Practically indefensible. It would be helpful getting in but hell for anyone trying to hold off an assault.

"Where do you think he has them?" Felipe whispered.

"Inside. You said there are two elevators. He probably has them there. How many have you seen?"

"Usually two."

"Armed with what?"

"AKs and sidearms. Nothing heavy."

"How many stories is it?"

"Fifteen. The station is on the thirteenth."

"No," Jorge said. "You've got to be kidding."

"*Ay*, you and the gypsy both? When you're my age you'll understand there's no such thing as luck. There's just what is and what is not."

"What else is in the building?"

"Offices, mostly foreign trade. Canadians, the French."

"No apartments?"

"None."

Across the street, the merengue ended and the crowd clapped. A rock song came on, big guitars and a thumping backbeat—actually a jingle urging them to drink Pacifico beer. Jorge thought he could see the DJ inside a large booth, a boom mike at face level. He wished he had his night-vision glasses.

"Is this normal," he asked, "or some special event?"

"Friday night the young people come out to listen to Bustus Domecq. He does the gum advertisements—have you seen them? Very clever. He dances with a mirror until there are two of him and then they can't agree on who will lead. There are rumors he's with us, but he's such a big star they can't do anything to him."

"Will he be here Monday?"

"No, he's the night man. We'll have the funny one, upstairs."

"And the armory's to our left."

"At the end of the block."

"What do you think?" Jorge asked him.

"About what?"

"About the whole thing."

"It's not impossible," the old man said.

They both looked across the street. A rap song started, and the dancers waved their hands in the air. In the booth, Bustus Domecq was spinning on his stool.

"At the same time," Felipe said, "it's not very probable either."

"I agree," Jorge said.

"In any case, it will be a surprise."

Jorge was about to agree again when they heard the scouring rush and scream of a fighter jet above. Some of the dancers stopped to look up. They waited for an explosion but there was nothing.

"Ours?" Felipe said.

"Maybe an old Phantom," Jorge said, though it was impossible to tell. It was better to let the old man hope. He wasn't even sure what they were running out of Honduras anymore. He'd seen retooled MiGs, and once an ancient Iranian F-14 with hiccupping Pratt & Whitney engines. They were magicians, those supply guys. It was scary what they could get their hands on—and what the Company wanted you to do with it.

"Yes," Felipe said, "an F-4. That's what hit the bridge in Segovia last week. Maybe it's the same one."

"I doubt it," Jorge said. "They have a lot of them."

The fighter cut back over the city, strakes screeching, and Jorge could tell it was a MiG. He wondered if the old man knew the difference.

"We should get back," Felipe said. "What else do you need to see?"

"Everything," Jorge said.

As they climbed through the jungle in the dark, a man ordered them to halt. His voice was a hiss, as if he didn't want to be heard. "Who goes?" They heard the bolt of an automatic jack back, then clash forward. He was somewhere in the brush above them.

"Friends," Felipe said, stepping in front of Jorge as if to protect him.

"Friends of whom?"

"Of Aurelio. Don't you know old Felipe?"

"What's the password?"

"We come from the city."

"I know," the man said in the dark. "You come from the station. I still need the password."

"Is that you, César?" Felipe asked.

"I asked you the password."

"There's no password, César," Felipe said. "You're having a joke."

The man jumped down from a tree and landed in the middle of the path. "You may pass," he said. He was gangly, almost a boy. In the moonlight, all Jorge could see was the glint of a gold tooth, a patch of close-cropped scalp.

"Son of a cow," Felipe said, and shoved the man.

"You have the heart of a mouse, old man. And you, *americano*, you have the voice of a fish."

Felipe shushed him.

"Pah," César said. "There's no one there. I've been here all night dying of boredom. I haven't eaten since this morning. Tell them that. Have them send Gloria down with something." He carelessly lit a cigarette and offered a hit to Jorge. It was a soldier's intimacy, not easily given, and Jorge could not refuse. "Little Ortega, is it true about the station?"

"What about it?"

"That it's suicide."

"Who says this?" Felipe asked. "Aurelio?"

"No one," the man said. "I have nothing against it. It's not my suicide. But beware those who would make it yours."

"What's that supposed to mean?" Jorge said.

César hesitated, scratching his bristly scalp as if he were thinking. "Just keep an eye on your plastique. I wouldn't want to be on the wrong end of it, if you understand me."

"I understand you," Jorge said. He took a last drag and handed the butt back. César stood aside and they climbed the trail again.

"Beans!" César called after them in the dark. "Tortillas!"

"Password?" Felipe taunted.

They listened for cavalry before crossing the broad path. At the beginning of the ravine they stopped to catch their breath. For the first time, Jorge saw it as a trap, a dead end. The camp was too convenient, too close to a major trail. After a while, the daily traffic of guards and scouting parties would wear a rut in the jungle floor, a map for the cavalry. He had yet to see the path in full daylight. He wondered how long they'd been in the cave. In a way, Aurelio was right; they'd have to leave here afterward. Maybe he was right about the whole thing. He could afford to be patient where Jorge couldn't.

He caught the old man watching him and tried to smile.

"César is a good man," Felipe said. "He speaks in riddles but always at bottom seriously."

"I thought he was just an asshole," Jorge said.

"He's that, yes, but a good man too. It's a strange combination in

29

him. He worries about Aurelio. We all do, even Luz, though she'll never admit it."

"Even to herself."

"I don't know that."

"What should we do about the plastique?" Jorge asked.

"We'll watch it—you, me and César."

"And Gloria."

"If you trust her."

"You don't?"

"I don't know her," the old man said.

"Why did you bring me here if you knew things were this bad?"

"I didn't have a choice. This is Aurelio's section. We have to deal with him."

"What about El Marichal?"

"He has his own section."

"Would he be better to deal with?"

"If this were his section, yes, but this isn't his section."

"So we're stuck," Jorge said. "Is that what you're telling me?"

"Yes," Felipe said. "Stuck. That's the perfect word for it."

.   .

THEY CLIMBED SOPPING up from the pool to the mouth of the cave, where a light poked out from the edge of a blanket hung to cover the opening. Jorge's pack leaned against the rock wall, a canvas thrown over it.

"Wait," Jorge whispered to Felipe, and knelt.

The canvas was dewy, a fallen drop tickling his fingers. He popped the snaps to reveal the locks holding the flap down. He remembered the combinations by seeing the players in his mind, their faces bringing back the numbers on their jerseys—Vada Pinson, Tony Perez, Manny Sanguillen. During spring training, his father used to take a week of vacation and the two of them would drive north to watch the great ones play on diamonds ringed with chain-link fence, infields hard as plaster. In the motel, his father drank whiskey from a plastic bathroom cup, sat propped up against the headboard and watched TV with his shoes off while Jorge drifted into sleep. He always brought his gun, shoved in his shoulder holster, and Jorge liked to pretend they were criminals on the lam. His mother was in Iowa somewhere, living with a sister. At breakfast they laid out the schedule and checked who was pitching, picked which games they wanted to see. "Ah, the great Cedeno," his father said, feeding his excitement, but when the waitress came his smile shrank and vanished as if happiness were an effort. His basement face returned, slack and unguarded, off-duty, the years of exile and disappointment plain and terrifying to the boy Jorge had been.

"So," Felipe asked, "is it okay?"

"I want to make sure."

He threw the flap open and dug beneath the cigarettes and the clean chinos and down along the hard wall of the Prick-60. The battery case was there. To really check it he'd have to haul everything out, but he already felt a little paranoid, and César didn't strike him as reliable. Tomorrow, he thought, just to be sure. His hand grazed the broken-in leather of his holster and he slipped the pistol out and fit it into the pocket of the windbreaker. Better safe, his father would say.

"It's fine," he told the old man, and buckled it up again and snapped the locks on. He motioned for Felipe to lead, then hefted the pack and followed him in, stooping as the old man lifted the blanket aside.

The light was blinding, the air smoky and stale, full of cooking oil and cigarettes and red peppers. A transistor radio chattered, spilling out the same music they'd heard downtown—the Bustus Domecq show. Rafael and Aurelio sat in rusted folding chairs around a gouged card table; with them were two men Jorge had never met. In back, Gloria and Luz were tasting something from a pot. When Luz looked up, Gloria saw him and smiled.

The men were playing poker, using small-caliber rounds as chips. One of the men wore a red do-rag like a Liberty City Blood; he was young, almost girlish, except for a brushburn running the length of his nose, as if someone had tried to file it off. The other was gray and clerklike, with thick glasses and several extra chins lapping at the bandanna around his sweaty neck. They both looked him over like gunfighters.

"I thought you were going to leave that outside," Aurelio said, pointing his cards at the pack.

"The damp is bad for it."

"And an explosion's good for us?" Rafael asked.

"I don't like it in the cave," Aurelio said, and chipped in a .22 round.

"It's away from the fire," Jorge said. "Here, have some cigarettes. They're more likely to kill you."

Aurelio looked at him as if he were going to speak again, then took them. The two strangers watched the Marlboros as if they were enchanted.

"Like some?" Jorge asked.

"Please," the gray one said.

"Thank you, Ortega," the young one with the do-rag said, and lit up. He was Hector, who had been on guard above the cave. The other was Teófilo; he warned Jorge prissily that he didn't like to be called Teo.

Gloria brought over a plate of roasted peppers and some kind of braised meat, and the men started in on it with their hands, smoking between bites. Iguana, she said, provided by Rafael. She brushed her front against Jorge as she passed, her breasts nudging him, and Rafael choked, laughing.

"You better eat," he joked. "You'll need your strength tonight."

"He's jealous," Hector with the do-rag said, and gray Teófilo chuckled.

"Oh, no no no," Rafael said, mock-serious, "it's good luck, they say, sleeping with an ugly woman."

For a moment no one spoke, only the radio going on. It was a test, Jorge thought. So much of the job was this kind of schoolyard bullshit.

"*I* don't think she's ugly," he finally said. He'd wanted it to be a threat, a challenge, but it came out more like a defense, halfhearted at that, and now he was mad. He bumped the back of Rafael's chair and looked down at him. "Do you really have so little honor?"

"I intended no disrespect," Rafael said, suddenly repentant, attempting to shrug it off.

"He has a gypsy's honor," Aurelio said. "It's like a communist's heart—it needs a microscope to be seen."

"Just like his privates," Gloria called from the back, and they all roared, even Rafael, and Jorge was forced to join in. It was a game, that was all, nothing to get upset about, and yet he was. It was Catalina again, all the old stuff bubbling up. It was why he was no longer part of a team, why he'd become expendable, shunted off to Forbes.

33

"Come get your *sopa*, lazy ones," Luz called, and the men laid their cards down.

It was black bean soup, thick and steaming, with chunks of onion. Gloria ladled it into empty cans. Felipe was the first in line, then Rafael. For a moment Aurelio disappeared, then came back inside, ducking under the blanket. He stood behind Jorge, stinking of rum.

"César wanted us to bring him something," Jorge remembered.

"After you eat," Luz ordered Gloria, who nodded. The bruises around her eyes seemed darker in the firelight, ghoulish. Her nose broke to one side, the tip a flattened nub like a prizefighter's. She wasn't ugly, he thought, just ruined. It was nothing to joke about.

As she ladled out a portion for Jorge, she looked at him accusingly. She leaned in close over the steaming can, as if to give him a kiss, to tell him a secret.

"You don't defend me," she whispered. "I'm my own, no one else's."

He apologized, unsure what to say next.

"*Vámonos,*" Aurelio said behind him, "I'm starving," and Jorge went back to the table.

He secretly watched her eat. While the rest of them were hunched over their cans, she crossed her legs above the knee and sat back, spine rigid, bringing the spoon to her lips. In her posture she had the confidence of a model, the arrogant indolence of privilege or hard-fought accomplishment, and he wondered where she had come from, what kind of life. He imagined different families for her—peasants and bureaucrats, warehouse managers, cook's helpers. And their house, was it a concrete-block hovel with a tin roof or a villa with a swimming pool overlooking the harbor? Did her mother drive a Mercedes or switch the muddy ass of a goat? She finished and fixed a can for César, threw a shawl on and ducked under the blanket and out into the night, and he thought that she'd begun to work on him. He was surprised it took so little. It was a bad sign.

When they'd finished, Hector the Blood took the cans down to the pool and rinsed them out. The poker game was over, the table cleared. Luz had joined the men, smoking, and the room had gone quiet. The rum was missing, and someone had turned off the little transistor. It was as if they were waiting to begin a meeting none of them wanted to attend. Jorge sat down beside her. Finally Hector came back inside. He began to set the cans out on a dish towel, but Luz told him to leave them and he came and sat down by the obese Teófilo. With his gray skin and three-day whiskers he looked like a manatee. And Hector, a wiry pirate with his scar. Mutt and Jeff, Jorge thought. It was a leader's trick, remembering your men's names, one he wasn't good at. Hector and Teófilo, Laurel and Hardy. Hector the Pirate, Teófilo the Manatee. There would be more, or so he hoped.

"All right," Aurelio said. "Has everything been explained sufficiently?"

"Has what been explained?" Felipe asked.

"The *americano's* plan."

"Well enough," Felipe said.

"Who's in favor of it?" Aurelio asked.

Felipe looked to Jorge, puzzled. Luz gave him the same look.

"I'm against it," Aurelio said. "I don't think it's good for us."

"Then we'll do it without you," Jorge said. "We'll miss your abilities."

"Who misses a coward?" Felipe said.

"What did you say, old man?" Aurelio said. His face was red and he was sweating.

"I said nothing to you."

Jorge looked to Luz. So far she'd been silent. He let his hand trail down the front of his windbreaker and into the pocket where the pistol waited. His thumb found the safety and slipped it off. It wasn't the way he wanted to do things, but still, it was his job.

"Listen to me," Aurelio said. "We do best when we plan our own operations. In Arriaga, have we ever lost a man?"

"Should I go to El Marichal?" Jorge asked.

"You'll go to no one. You'll do nothing to jeopardize the section."

"It's not a choice," Jorge said. "Forbes will be here Monday at dawn, with or without us."

"Without us then. We'll be needed even more after that. Do any one of you trust the Americans to succeed? I don't. Where will we be then?"

The rest of them contemplated it. Jorge slipped the safety back on. If he was lost here, he thought, then he was lost. He would have to find others, and there was little time.

35

"No," Luz finally said. "The Americans don't care for us."

"There," Aurelio said, pleased.

"But I care," Luz continued. "And not so long ago you cared too. I don't know what has happened to you. You've become someone who cares only for his own safety."

"What are you saying?"

"I'm saying I am for the Ortega. I am for the station. I am for Cuba."

"Then you betray me." He turned and spat in the dirt.

"I merely speak my heart."

"I'm for the station," Teófilo the Manatee said flatly, as if there were no question.

"I'm not for the station," Rafael said, "and I'm not for Cuba, but I'm with Luz."

"I'm with Luz," Hector the Pirate echoed.

"Idiots!" Aurelio said. "Think! You're talking with your bowels instead of your brains. They'll hunt us through the mountains like deer. It's not Benítez anymore, it's Clemente. He has the brain of a general. Ask the old man if I'm lying."

"It is Clemente," Felipe admitted, "but I believe the Americans are serious this time."

No, Jorge wanted to say, it's a mistake to think so, but he said nothing. For a second he wondered if the Company had sent him here not to help but to scuttle the revolution—if the people above Forbes wanted them to succeed only so far. There were games inside of games, like a catcher jawing all nine innings with the umpire, telling jokes, putting things in his mind early on, subtle expectations, promises.

"It doesn't matter if they're serious," Luz said. "We're serious."

"Do you hear what you're saying?" Aurelio screamed. "Don't you understand what will happen?"

"What will happen must happen."

"You'll throw away all of our work. You'll all be killed—for what?"

"Shut up," Luz said. "You don't frighten us with your cowardly talk."

"Cowardly? How is it cowardly to see the future? It's not a question of cowardice. Doesn't anyone see this?"

No, Jorge thought, only the two of us. Perhaps Luz.

"It's foolishness," Aurelio pleaded. "Listen to your *comandante*."

Luz laughed. "And who's that?"

"Who planned the raid on the substation—and the checkpoint? Who found this cave?"

"Who let the *blanco* go into the city? Haven't you been listening? They follow me. I command here."

"I should shoot you and the *americano* both."

Jorge slid his hand into his pocket again. Too late, he thought. He was getting sloppy.

"You should but you won't," Luz said. "You've even lost the courage to be a murderer."

"Go to the devil," Aurelio said, "both of you." He reached for his back pocket and Jorge rose and showed him the pistol.

Everyone sat back, as if waiting for Jorge to shoot him.

Aurelio smiled. "This is the man you trust." Easily, he pulled out a silver flask. He uncapped it and drank. "As you see, I'm no coward, and no traitor. You'll see I'm right. Here I disgrace myself to save your lives, and you have no gratitude. It's a sad thing, a man as myself. It will be me and Clemente then, I can see it. You'd rather not consider the future."

"I have a future?" Felipe said.

"Laugh, old *cabrón*," Aurelio said. "Go ahead, I won't listen to it." He pocketed his flask and stood. He kept his eyes locked on Jorge's, bumping him as he passed, then flung the blanket aside and stepped out into the night.

Jorge thumbed the safety on and slid the pistol back into his windbreaker. He sat down.

"That was stupid," Luz said. "I risk everything and look what you do to me. We're supposed to believe in you now?" He could see the rest of them felt the same, all but Felipe, who thought it comical.

"I'm sorry. I didn't know what he was reaching for."

"That's because you don't know him—you don't know *us*. And obviously we don't know you at all."

The blanket parted, and they turned to see Gloria enter with a can in her hand.

"Aurelio's out there drinking," she reported.

"Well," Luz said, apologetic, "he's got reason enough."

JORGE DREW THE blanket aside and stepped out into the heavy night air. There was no wind, and he could smell the jungle—the rot of moss and fungus. It took a minute for the stars to appear, as if only now their light was finding its way through the canopy. The steps were empty, no glowing ember of Aurelio's cigarette. The pool was calm, only the trickle of a rill going over the dam.

"Idiot," Jorge said. It was a shame—the only one with any tactical sense, and now they couldn't depend on him. It happened; after a number of operations people became cautious, weighed the gains against the risks. They got smarter, basically. Though Jorge had known since Aurelio had shown him the radios, he had not wanted it to come to this. But that was war—there was no faking it, no pleasant way to beg off. You were either in or you were out, and Aurelio was out.

He stood there contemplating the night sky, his mind ticking off the possibilities. The moon was a bright scythe.

At least the weather's holding up, he thought.

Inside, someone strummed a guitar, and then Rafael sang in memorized phonetic English:

Is a star out tonight
I don't know if it's cloudy or bright

His voice cracked trying to find *bright,* and there was laughter and the hollow clunk of the guitar against someone's knee. The same chords came again, but slower, fuller, as if this player knew the real fingerings.

Are the stars out tonight? someone sang in a sweet high alto, and it took a moment for Jorge to recognize gray Teófilo behind the voice. The Manatee singing.

As he looked up to answer the question, the flap flew open and Rafael came out with a cigarette and steaming coffee in a tin can. "Ah," he said, "the brave Ortega."

"Ah, Rafael with the voice of a fish."

"I spoke," the gypsy said, "when it was my time."

"Your time always seems to come too late."

"I'm a gypsy—my time is my own business and none of yours. And you're one to talk of lateness." He tugged savagely at his cigarette, and Jorge was unsure if they were still joking.

"Where do you think he went?" Jorge asked.

"He's crying to his beauties. His radios. He goes to the cave like a brothel. It's a joke on Luz."

"Would he go against us?"

"Tonight?"

"I don't like the way he left."

Rafael shrugged. "César's there if he has any plans." He offered Jorge his cup, and Jorge took a sip—the coffee was strong and uncut. As he handed him the can, Rafael took his wrist like a confidant. He spoke low, as if the rest of their conversation had been false, just small talk. "Why didn't you shoot him?"

"There was no need," Jorge whispered.

"You'll have to eventually, you know that."

"I don't think so."

"Why do you think Luz sent the girl out? He doesn't have any friends left. They're all dead."

"Then why was Luz angry with me?"

"I have to tell you this? A man doesn't take his gun out to put it away. You think he'll forget? A coward remembers everything."

"I was about to and then I thought better of it."

"Yes, we all saw. Next time don't think. Do it now, when he comes back."

"He's still valuable," Jorge said, not quite believing it himself.

"Sooner or later," Rafael said. "It will be worse later. We only have two days."

"I'm aware of that."

"Don't make it difficult."

Inside, the song ended, to applause.

"It's already difficult," Jorge said. In the silence, his voice sounded loud.

"No," the gypsy said, "it's simple." He flipped his cigarette in a long arc, the black plane of the pool suddenly catching it. He turned and lifted the blanket, paused dramatically, looking back. "You *make* it difficult."

INSIDE THE CAVE, Jorge sat on a hard folding chair at the card table, next to Luz. She and Gloria were filling shotgun shells with rusted screws and nuts, and Jorge was crimping them with an old loader. It was late, and they each had a finger of rum. Aurelio hadn't come back yet, and he could see Luz was worried, but no one said anything. It was just the three of them in the cave. She'd sent Hector and Teófilo back to their posts, Rafael had gone down the mountain to relieve César, and Felipe was asleep by the fire.

On the table sat a stained grape crate filled with cast-off fasteners and jagged scrap, and beside it a cardboard box of finished shells. They had a sawed-off, a pretty Ithaca with ducks carved on the stock; they'd stolen it from some bureaucrat's hunting camp. It was a shame, Jorge thought, a lovely bird gun like that. Luz picked the shell, Gloria filled it, Jorge crimped it.

"It's odd," Luz said. "El Marichal's usually very prompt."

"Maybe he's busy with something more important," Gloria offered.

"If he doesn't come tonight, we'll have to make a trip to see him tomorrow. I'm sure that word of the Ortega has reached him."

"He probably already knows the details of the landing," Jorge said. "Everyone else does."

"That's Felipe," Luz said, tipping her head toward the old man in his bedroll. "There's a touch of the Catalan in him. He'd rather talk than make love."

"Señor Oaks refused to speak with him," Gloria said. "Not that he could speak much." She pushed a bent wing nut into her shell and tamped it down with her pinky.

"Actually you're the first they've sent us who can speak," Luz said. "It's helpful. Are there many like you?"

"With Forbes, not many," Jorge said. "But in America there are. Miami's full of men who will fight."

"We all know of your grandfather," Gloria said, "what of your father?"

"He's dead."

"*Lo siento.*" I'm sorry.

"As I am," Luz said. "Though he wouldn't have been that old, surely."

"It was an accident. He was a policeman."

"A brave man," Luz said, "like his father before him."

"Yes," Jorge said, wondering if it was a lie.

"And your mother?" Gloria asked.

"Dead also. The cancer."

"Heaven protect you," Luz said.

"Brothers, sisters?"

"None."

"Cousins?"

"Many."

"Thank the Holy Mother," Luz said. "To be without family is an affliction."

"Where is yours?" he asked.

"Dead or in prison. I fight to release them someday."

"And yours?" he asked Gloria.

"My grandmother is in America—Syracuse, Nueva York. My mother is dead. My father I don't know. I lived with my aunt until the *guardia* came and took us. There was a revolver in the house, from before the war. My aunt received ten years. I received five, though I'd never seen this weapon. When I was released, I came to the mountains with César."

"No brothers and sisters?"

"I have a brother Jorge."

"Honestly," Jorge asked.

"He's in the *federale* just as I was, but for drugs. He's been there since I was a child."

There was a silence like shame, and they concentrated on the shells. There wasn't much left, just a sandy residue of metal shavings, a few stray ball bearings.

"Now that we're all cheered up," Luz said, and took a slug of rum. In the corner, the fire flickered. Jorge glanced at the blanket, wondering how soon César and his gold teeth and crew cut would appear. He needed to see him again to memorize his name, develop the minimum intimacy he needed to lead him. It was impossible to ask someone you didn't know to die for you. Even raw politics wasn't enough. Aurelio was proof.

He looked at Luz, picking through the dully colored shell casings.

"May I speak honestly?" Jorge asked her, and Gloria looked up from the grape crate.

"If you must," Luz said.

"The gypsy said I should have gone ahead—"

"No," Luz interrupted, "he's wrong. It's a weakness in him, the distrust."

"But if I must," Jorge started.

"Then you will," she said. "There was no call for it, and you saw that."

"If he goes against us—"

"He won't. I know him. He's past being for or against things. If you expect nothing from him, you'll be fine." She passed a shell to Gloria, who tipped the crate and pinched the dregs from one corner. Jorge fit it into the crimper and jacked the handle.

"Well," Luz said, stacking the last shell with the others, "at least we accomplished something tonight." She lifted the box and lugged it across the cave to a natural shelf in the wall.

"You must be tired," Gloria said. "You've done a lot today." Her lips barely moved, like a ventriloquist's.

"It *has* been a long day," he agreed.

"You should sleep outside," she said. "The air's better there."

"I'm not afraid of Aurelio."

"I didn't mean to imply you were. It's just nicer outside."

"With the bugs."

"I have netting if you like."

Over her shoulder, he could see Luz pretending to mess with the shells, wasting time until they finished their conversation.

"It's a beautiful night," Gloria argued, and he could see that she'd win, just as he knew that later, in her arms, he'd see Catalina. Often it seemed to him that he woke from one bad dream only to find himself in another, and yet they were all true, part of a continuity he lacked the strength to escape—unlike, he thought, his father.

"It is," he said.

IN THE DARK HE COULDN'T see her. They were above the cave, the smell of the dying fire reaching them. He hadn't forgotten Aurelio, and had the pistol beneath the flap of his pack, the safety off. She was hard from work, her shoulders bony. She gave him her bottom, but Jorge turned her over, as if he wanted to see her. He knew she wanted him to kiss her, and he tried to forget the gaps between her teeth, his tongue grazing them like icebergs. Her hair smelled of cooking oil and smoke, and there was salt on her neck. She cupped the back of his head and took him to her breast. He could hear her heart tripping, her gasps of passion. He thought he couldn't match her honestly, but once they'd begun he found himself interested, even hungry. Ferns brushed against his ribs, rustling. He hardly saw Catalina, just a glimpse of her in the tin shack at the base camp. It was enough. She was above him, shirtless but still in her bra, her crucifix swinging as she rocked against him.

Jorge knew when it was from—the day before the power lines. The general strike had already been called, they were only waiting for orders from the city. The sun was up, a gecko basking in the blazing square above the cot. In the corner his radio was open, the empty frequency bathing them in static. She reached behind herself to unhook her bra, smiling at his helplessness, and her breasts came free. Catalina, *te amo.*

And suddenly he was back in the jungle, in the dark, pouring into the faceless woman beneath him, his breath heavy with onions and rum. It was like Miami, the ugly make-believe of one-night stands— condoms tossed out of moving cars, cheap water-damaged apartments, dogs barking down cracked alleys. He felt he had been cheated of something, though he knew it was untrue, that he was being selfish. He wanted Catalina back. Sometimes, like now, lying down, he missed the nightmares.

"You think of another," Gloria asked.

"No."

"You are mine," she asked sadly, throwing a leg over him. "You have come so far to be with me."

"Yes."

"What else?" she said. "Tell me."

Around them, tree frogs peeped.

"You're sweet," he said.

"Say my name, Ortega."

"Gloria."

"Tell me I'm beautiful."

"You are," he said. "I could see that the first time."

"I'm not really like this."

"I know."

"They can fix it, yes? In Miami, they can fix everything."

It was possible, he thought—all but the rage in her eyes, the impossibility of forgiveness.

"Yes," he said.

"It's ridiculous. In the *federale* I gave them everything except my face. Always I saved it. My hands, my arms, my back—they beat me with strips cut from tires, with their boots, but always I was careful. Now it's all lost."

"I can still see it," Jorge said.

"You're kind, but no. Luz says it's just pride and I'll defeat it. She doesn't say how."

From below came splashing, someone cutting through the pool, and Jorge's hand flashed to the pack and gripped the pistol. Gloria clutched his arm. He took her hand, and they waited.

Under the canopy, a bat creaked past, black against the moon. Jorge held his breath, listening for the crack of a twig, the swish of a leaf.

The tree frogs peeped.

"He's gone to sleep," Gloria whispered, but still he waited another minute before agreeing. He put the gun away and rolled over.

Her hands ran down his belly and found him, started working him up, the friction delicious.

"Will he go against us?" Jorge asked. "Luz says no."

"At the checkpoint he was very brave, but that was months ago."

"And now?"

"Who am I to say?"

"We have two days," Jorge said. "I need a better answer than that."

She let go of him and sighed, as if he'd ruined the mood. "I'm not Luz, I owe him no loyalty. I have no confidence in him—no one does, not even Hector. But I wouldn't kill him. You need Luz too much for that. The best thing is to watch him. Make sure he doesn't leave camp like tonight, and keep him away from his radios. Don't give him anything important to do."

"You'll help me?"

"For a price," she said, and rolled on top of him.

"What price is that?"

"You take me when you leave. To Miami."

It would never happen, he thought, so he was not really lying when he said, "If I can."

"If I can," she mimicked, riding him now. "What a promise! You will. I'll make you."

"How?" Jorge asked.

She laughed and flung her hair back, and before Jorge could stop himself he was with Catalina again, the day before the power lines, and none of this—none of this—was real.

"That's how," Gloria said, "and that, and that," but far-off, like the cries of the children kicking the soccer ball outside the window, lost in the static of an open frequency.

47

CHAPTER

THE FIRST SQUADRON of helicopters woke him, going over in a high diamond formation, thudding south down the valley toward Santa Rosa. It wasn't quite light out. Gloria was gone. His pistol was still there, and he grabbed it and lay still in the bedroll as if it would make a difference. The blips moved through the leaves of the canopy.

They were Kamov Werewolves, top of the line, their stumpy tail booms a giveaway; their rotors chopped at the air with a slightly higher pitch than the U.S. Hueys with their flat bap-bap-bap. The Nam vets he'd worked with in Honduras knew them from miles away, could tell just from the sound when they needed engine work. He knew the Fidelistas had some, he was just surprised they'd send them down here. These were too high to be recon; they were probably coming from Arriaga, headed for Clemente's airfield.

He rose and hauled on the chinos Felipe had lent him, only to hear a second squadron. His instinct was to drop to his bedroll, though he knew they couldn't see him. It was the same formation.

"Chill," he said, and got up again, braced for another wave.

It was ballsy, he thought; they were low enough for a small SAM to take them down. Maybe it was bait. He wondered if the Company had supplied El Marichal with anything.

Aurelio, Luz and the gypsy had gathered at the cave mouth, their hair flattened, clumps jutting out. They peered up through the canopy as if there were more.

"Is this normal?" Jorge asked.

"No," Luz said, but nothing else. Her breath smelled of sleep. She seemed stunned, watching the skies like someone waiting for lightning to strike.

"I've never seen so many," Rafael said. "What are they?"

Jorge told him.

"I don't know them," Aurelio said, "and I know all the helicopters here."

"How many does Clemente have at the airfield?" Jorge asked.

Luz and the gypsy turned to Aurelio, who was still looking sky-ward, concentrating on the rotors slapping. The noise seemed to be dwindling, then it grew again, moved closer, joined by the whine of turbines.

"Inside," Aurelio ordered. Jorge wanted to say there was no reason to unless they had thermal imaging, but he didn't want to argue—it was too small a point, and it was early, there was too much to be done. He followed Rafael in, ducking under the blanket.

Felipe and Gloria sat at the card table, playing a game and drinking coffee from their tin cans. She smiled at Jorge, then covered her mouth with her cards. He checked Luz but she was at the blanket, peeking out. Everything still smelled of cooking oil, greasy onions. It wasn't quite five-thirty by Jorge's watch.

"Four more, eh?" Felipe said. "That makes twelve."

"How many does Clemente have at the airfield?" Aurelio asked the old man.

Felipe had to think, scratching a bushy eyebrow with the corner of his cards. "Nine before these."

"What kind are they?" Jorge asked.

"Six Hinds with rocket launchers, and three light ones with just machine guns. I can draw a map of the hangars."

"There's no need," Luz said. "It's the number I'm worried about."

"An insane number," said Rafael. "And new ones."

"It's not good," Aurelio agreed.

"They can't win with just helicopters," Jorge said. "It's a city. They need men. Felipe?" He nodded toward the blanket.

The old man laid his cards down and stood up.

"You can't talk here?" Aurelio said. "I'm not to be trusted now— the section commander?"

"You're not in command here," Luz said. "I am."

Aurelio wilted in front of her. He turned to Jorge as if he were to blame, not in anger but pleading, and Jorge could see he'd given up.

"I mean no disrespect, Don Aurelio. I trust you like I trust myself. I have my way of commanding, you have yours."

"I don't like your way."

"It's of no importance what you think," Luz said.

"Please," Jorge said, to stop them. He felt sorry for Aurelio, and he couldn't afford a lovers' quarrel. "I'll speak with you later. Right now I have to talk to the *viejo.*"

He turned, and Felipe drew the blanket aside.

Jorge led the old man up the slope to his bedroll. The sun was rising, the jungle beginning to steam. He checked his watch: they were less than forty-eight hours away and nothing had been done yet. He tried to think of what he needed to do first, but it all came to him in a flood—the *guardia,* the elevators, the engineer. They'd have to rush the DJ while a song played.

"What do you need me for?" Felipe asked.

"I want you to watch the road from Arriaga. Make a record of everything going into Santa Rosa. Trucks, tanks, artillery—everything."

"What if there's nothing?"

"There won't be nothing, trust me."

"How long should I stay?"

"Rafael's going into the city. When he's done there, he'll relieve you. It shouldn't be more than five or six hours."

"I'll miss lunch."

"Then get something and take it with you. Go. And send the gypsy out."

The old man made his way down the slope gingerly, a hand out, catching lianas, and in a minute Rafael trudged up, eating a pomegranate with his bayonet. His lips were red and he spat out the pulp as he went, a stray seed caught in his muttonchops. What a crew, Jorge thought. No wonder Oaks did everything himself. Still, it was a mistake, one he'd avoid. Men didn't win wars, Forbes said; organization did. Somehow he'd find a way to match them up with what he needed to get done. He always had in the past.

"Finally," said Rafael, "you ask me to your bed. The Gloria isn't enough for you, eh? Don't tell that to César, he'll shoot you."

"They're together?" Jorge asked.

"In his mind they are. You can see it in his eyes, for months now. Then you come—the great Ortega—and she lies down like cane at the harvest. It's a mystery."

"He'll be angry."

"So what? He is a nonentity, a man made entirely of beans. Why do you call me away from my food?"

"I need you to watch the guards at the station. I need to know how many there are and when they change shifts."

"That will take all day and all night."

"I'm only concerned with the morning shift."

"I'll need a watch."

Jorge undid his.

"A formidable watch," Rafael said.

"It's my father's." It wasn't, but he'd lost too many this way.

"I'll take great care."

"When you're done, relieve the old man and watch the road for me."

"How long?"

"Until dark."

"It's too much work for one man. Send Hector, or Teófilo."

"No," Jorge said. "You. It's *muy importante* and you're my best man, for lack of others."

"*Gracias,* Ortega. You are my finest *comandante.*"

"Go finish your breakfast. I want you there by six-thirty."

"And what will you do while I slave like a mule?"

"Go visit El Marichal."

"Ah," Rafael said. "Good. He's not worthless like our one. Who else is going?"

"Not him. Luz will make sure."

"Who will watch him?"

"You tell César on your way down and we'll tell Hector above."

"If he wants to leave, he will. Eventually you'll have to choose."

"Luz says no."

"That's Luz. Ask your Gloria."

"I have," Jorge said.

"And the *viejo?*" Rafael looked at him and understood. "This is democracy, no—what we fight for."

"No," Jorge said, "this is war. Now go, I need you there now."

Rafael chucked the pomegranate into the jungle. "Mark me," he said, "the gypsy sees," and walked away.

Jorge policed his bedroll and secured his pack, then hiked down to the cave. It was already hot, the mosquitoes worrying his wet neck. He hoped Luz had come up with something harmless for Aurelio to do, and for an instant he wondered if the landing was a diversion, if they were to be sacrificed. Forbes would cut him loose in a minute, it was part of the bargain. And it was like that all the way to the top. They loved the Pope coming, and the fact that Castro was dead, but beyond that they saw no urgency. Officially they had no stake in Cuba, and now without the Soviets it was true unofficially too, all but a few old throwbacks in the Company trying to shrug off their Bay of Pigs albatross. But wasn't that him? His father would laugh at his naiveté, joining up with the same people who'd betrayed them so many times before.

There was nothing to be gained thinking that way, and he shook it off. This wasn't some late-night Little Havana bull session over dominos. This wasn't theoretical. He was here, where he'd always wanted to be, and it made him happy.

Hadn't his father taken pride in his life, the honorable part of it? One of the good guys, he called himself, and had the medals to prove it. He'd saved lives, held the hands of the dying. After everything, Jorge thought, this was his chance.

The pool was still, the rocks at the bottom glinting, water purling over the dam. He pulled the blanket aside and ducked into the cool dimness of the cave.

A tiny man he'd never seen sat at the table with Luz, discussing something. He had on a straw cowboy hat and a bandanna rolled about his neck. His skin was dark from the sun, and he had a ridiculously big mustache shaped like a comb. His T-shirt said *Georgetown Hoyas* above a jowly bulldog in a spiked collar.

"Francisco," Luz said, pointing to Jorge. "Tell the Ortega what you've heard."

"*Salud*," the man said with an officious nod, and Jorge returned it. "I come from Segovia. The rumor in the north is that we're preparing an offensive."

"Where?" Jorge asked.

"Here in Santa Rosa, in the mountains."

"Where did you hear this?"

"Everywhere," Francisco said. "In the cafés, in the brothels—wherever there are soldiers. The city isn't safe. At every street corner they ask for your papers."

"Is the airfield busy?" Luz asked.

"Tremendously. These are the helicopters you see. They arrived two days ago. And there are tanks and antiaircraft guns behind them, I hear, and many men. There's a troop train from La Habana arriving in the morning."

Well, that was it, Jorge thought. If they brought in ground troops it would be impossible. Forbes could bomb them all day and it wouldn't matter.

"What else do you hear?"

"There's talk of the radio station of Bustus Domecq, that we'll try to seize it."

Aurelio laughed by the fire. "He's joking, obviously."

"Don't laugh at me," the little man said fiercely. "I've been stopped five times since leaving Segovia."

"He apologizes," Luz said. "But it's incredible news. Have you spoken with El Marichal?"

"I come to you first. They say Clemente has placed a bounty on the head of the *americano.*"

"What *americano?*" Gloria said.

"Him," Francisco said, jerking a thumb at Jorge. "You have another?"

"Do they use his name?" Luz asked.

"No, just "the '*americano.*'"

"I hope it's not too large," Rafael said, feigning temptation. "I could use a new pair of boots."

"Did you bring any good news?" Luz asked.

"One thing. An American plane has been coming over every morning at seven for a week now. Very far up. Even in the binoculars it's a speck."

"How do you know it's American?" Jorge asked.

"My Vietnamese friend says it is, and he saw many in the war."

"And the government," Aurelio asked, setting a steaming plate of beans in front of him, "they can't see this plane?"

"*No se,*" Francisco said. Don't know. He dug in, then pulled back as if the beans were too hot. Gloria slid him her coffee and he guzzled some.

"So it's off," Aurelio said.

"What's off?" Luz said. "Nothing's off."

"They know," Aurelio said. "It's madness."

"Go tend the fire. I won't listen to you."

"Can't you check with your *generalissimo?*" Aurelio asked.

"Radio silence," Jorge explained. It was pointless; Forbes had spent years putting this together. Like every war, it wasn't a question of surprise but of will, how much you were prepared to lose. Forbes could afford to lose everything. For some weird reason the thought cheered Jorge, as if he knew the position. Nothing to lose.

"You see?" Luz said. "It's not a choice."

"I see," Aurelio said, nodding grimly. "That's the problem—I see everything clearly."

"It's true," Luz said, "you've become an old witch-woman," and he turned and went back to the fire.

Francisco stirred his beans and tucked in again, the brim of his straw hat dipping with each bite, his mustache wet. He ate without stopping, like a farmhand, which Jorge supposed he was. The rest of them watched as if it were a performance. Jorge wondered if the news had changed anything. Looking around the table at Rafael and Gloria and Luz, at Felipe wrapping his grilled onions in a scorched tortilla, he thought not. And just then they heard the long, soft approach of another squadron of helicopters.

CHAPTER

HE COUNTED TWENTY-FOUR of them, all Werewolves. Luz pretended to ignore them, but each time a wave passed over, she headed for the back of the cave, as if for safety. She sent Aurelio and Francisco to do a full operational on the old radios, which impressed Jorge. It in fact had to be done, and Aurelio seemed pleased that Jorge didn't insist on running the check himself.

There were only the three of them in the cave—Jorge, Gloria and Luz; Felipe and Rafael were on their way down the mountain. It would take a good part of the morning to reach El Marichal's. Jorge helped Gloria pack their lunches, their shoulders touching, then she took the dirtied plates and cans down to the pool. Luz stirred the ashes of the fire, separating the embers. They were only waiting for César to come up from below so there would be someone to guard Jorge's pack.

"You made love to her?" Luz asked.

"She made love to me."

"It's the same thing. But it's not love." She seemed bitterly sure, which offended him.

"How do you know?"

"You're not a boy," Luz said, kicking a glowing chunk with the toe of her boot. "One knows, always."

"Maybe I'm a boy then."

"Did you say you'd take her with you? That's what she asks all of them."

"I said I'd try."

"*Tonto!*" she cried, turning to him. "Stupid! Didn't I tell you? I'm going to need her after you're gone."

"I don't think I'm going to be leaving here," Jorge said.

Luz spat into the ashes. "I cry for you. *Americano!* You think of nothing but your own happiness."

"I thought it would be better for her if I said yes."

"So you say whatever you wish. You have no honor. Perhaps you're a boy after all."

"I saw no harm in it."

"No harm? Listen to me," she began, but before she could finish, the blanket drew back, letting in a slice of light, and Gloria ducked through with a net full of dripping dishes.

"César's here," she announced, and started pulling out the cans and drying them with a flowered dishtowel, setting them on the shelf in the wall.

"You know what I think," Luz told him calmly, as if they'd been having a sedate conversation. "We're agreed on that at least."

"Yes," he conceded, and went to help Gloria.

César came in with a Mac-10, wearing cammies. With his buzz cut and his gold tooth and a cigarette dangling from his lip, he looked like an extra in a cheap Vietnam movie. Gloria turned to the shelf so she wouldn't have to look at him. Jorge wondered where he'd come from—some sharecropper family shoved onto a collective, maybe cane people—and how he'd come to be with Gloria. What had he been to her, and what was he now?

"Little Ortega, did you see the pretty Werewolves?"

"How many did *you* count?" Jorge asked.

"Twenty-four. Think they're for us?"

"They still need men to hold the city."

"How many does Forbes have?" Though he spoke to Jorge, his eyes never left Gloria, and Jorge found himself moving to shield her.

"Even if I knew, I wouldn't tell you."

"Probably wise." He laid the gun down on the card table and swirled the remains of Jorge's coffee before taking a sip. "Where's the *comandante?*"

"With his beauties," Luz said. "And stop calling him that."

"I suppose you are the new *comandante.*"

"I am," Luz said.

"*Ay,* Santa Rosario preserve us. You have the wiles of the bull. Coward that he is, Aurelio still thinks like the rat."

"Do you trust him?" Gloria asked, and he looked to Luz.

"It's not a question of trust," César said. "It's a question of desperation."

"Shut up," Luz ordered. "This isn't a discussion. We're already late for El Marichal because of you."

"Come," Jorge said. "I'll show you where it is."

"I don't like it," César said outside, climbing the path above the cave mouth. "All this craziness. I'm beginning to think like Aurelio."

"How so?"

"I think the station's a mistake. They're getting ready for us. Something's gone wrong."

"Something's always wrong," Jorge said.

"Granted, but these are the first Werewolves I've seen here. If we have to fight with these odds, we need Aurelio. He can think sideways; Luz can only think straight ahead."

They reached the pack, secure under its canvas, the straps padlocked around the base of a banyan tree.

"And how do I think?" Jorge asked.

"I can't say. I don't know you."

"How should I think?" Jorge said. "If you were me."

"That's fair," César said, grimly amused. He looked up through the canopy at the almost white sky, then back at Jorge. "If I were you," he said, "I shouldn't think at all."

CHAPTER  10

THEY HIKED STRAIGHT UP the mountain until the jungle gave way to bare granite ridges streaked with bird dung and the sun was high above them. They followed the spine east, the land spreading dramatically on both sides. To the south, the sea lay blue and flat as a table, the horizon precise; to the north lay Arriaga, the canals and fields of cane laid out neatly, the palms like dots. Luz chose an overhang with a view down the valley, and they sat with their legs dangling over the edge and unwrapped their tortillas. Luz passed a slice of lime to squeeze over the strips of goat meat. Jorge's shirt stuck to him, but Gloria showed only a faint sheen above her lip. Both women had their hair tucked up under olive drab caps, a few wisps lilting. The goat was tough but spicy.

"How much further is it?" he asked.

"Two hours," Luz said, waving a hand down the valley.

Jorge went to check his watch but it was gone, with Rafael.

"We should have taken the horses," Gloria said.

"And go all the way around? This is safer, especially with the helicopters."

For a while they ate without speaking, passing a canteen between them. The rock was hot. A breeze chilled the wet hair on his neck. Far off, a sugar mill chuffed out toy clouds. It reminded him of the professor taking him up into the hills above San Salvador, the way the power lines crossed the valley, the towers endlessly repeating. They had to choose one to blow up. Catalina was afraid of heights, and crushed his hand.

"You think it'll work?" Gloria asked.

"What?" Luz said.

"The landing. You think it will succeed?"

"What a question," Luz said. "Ask him."

Gloria turned to him, and Jorge thought of what Luz had said about his own happiness.

"Who knows?" he said. "Anything can happen."

"Very comforting."

"It's the truth," Jorge said.

"That's all you can ask for," Luz said, but Gloria didn't seem convinced.

"You were supposed to say yes," she scolded him.

"*Qué va,*" Luz said, getting up. "Be glad. When a man tells you the truth it's a lucky day."

Gloria capped the canteen and stood. "It's sad. When I was beautiful, they lied to me."

"They still lie to you," Luz said. "It's just the Ortega is no good at it."

"Thank you," Jorge said.

"See? I insult him and he thanks me. This is the true *americano.*"

They policed the area and shouldered their packs. Luz had a walking stick. Gloria was in the middle. Jorge went to check his watch again, and sighed.

They stayed on the ridge for a few miles, at one point crossing a rope bridge above a sheer chasm. Far below, lodged in the rocks, lay a dead spider monkey, crows picking the skin off its back. Luz crossed herself, Gloria just shook her head.

"Anything can happen," she mimicked.

Later they stopped for water. The valley hadn't moved—the same plantations, the same mill shooting a white plume into the sky. Far asea, a dark wall of clouds smudged the horizon. Jorge tipped the canteen up and didn't mention it. Hurricane season was a month away.

There were no contingency plans for weather; they were on regardless.

"There it comes," Gloria said.

"It will pass," Luz said uncertainly, then snapped the canteen onto her belt and moved out.

Farther on, the mountain sloped down and the ridge widened and gave way to lush jungle again. Under the canopy the air was thick and smelled of orchids and standing water, and Jorge wished he'd brought more than just his pistol. Brush muscled in on both sides, the toothy leaves ripping at them. Luz slowed, her head bowed, intent on the trail. She stopped.

"Here." She pointed to an arrangement of cut vines on the ground. They were laid out like a tic-tac-toe board, in the center a clump of moss. "A key for today's password," she explained to Gloria.

The rest of the way was downhill. The trail split again and again, but Luz knew the way. Jorge tried to remember it in case something happened to her, but it was impossible. They came over a saddle and the land leveled out, changed to gently rolling foothills. They crossed a stream dammed with rocks, cut through a muddy stand of mangroves, and suddenly they were facing the valley floor, the cane head-high for miles.

Luz pointed to a shallow canal, and they sloshed through it, the water filling his boots, the mud sucking at them like gravity. With every step, tornadoes of bugs exploded from the surface. The cane rose wall-like on both sides. It was like being in a maze. Ahead, another canal crossed theirs, and Luz turned left.

"Stop," a man said, and the sight of an AK poked out of a brake, aimed at Luz's face. "Password."

"*Cepeda,*" she said, and the man lowered the muzzle and stepped out into the water and hugged Luz. He was heavy and had wraparound sunglasses and a little goatee and a gold chain around his neck. He looked like a saxophonist in a dance band; all he was missing was the bowling shirt.

"Gloria," he said, nodding respectfully.

"Pasquale," Luz said, "this is the Ortega."

"An honor," the big man said. "*Camarada,* may you enjoy the success your name portends." He led them into the cane, where there was a trail.

"See, Jorge," Gloria said. "Here is a man who knows how to speak."

"What a tongue," Luz said. "It's from sitting all day in the cane and reading poetry. Who do you have today?"

"The *inglés,* Lord Byron. *Muy romantico.*"

"You have some of your own for us?"

"Not today," Pasquale said. "We're busy with the preparations."

"Where's the old man?"

"At the command post."

"Where was he last night?"

"In Arriaga. He went to see the helicopters. You saw them?"

"All twenty-four."

Pasquale stopped and looked at her. "Thirty-six."

"Marvelous," Luz said.

Gloria turned to Jorge but said nothing.

They went on, the dried shoots rattling underfoot. Ahead, a ruined mill loomed, its tin roof rusted along the seams, the gutters buckled, a porch hanging off at a ridiculous angle. Vines and tangle covered the broken windows. A rusty chain bound a pair of large garage doors, but Pasquale slid a corrugated tin panel aside and led them in, whistling the same three notes until someone above answered.

The ground floor was cluttered with rusting machinery—conveyor belts aimed into chutes feeding giant hoppers. Above, on an open catwalk, stood a hunched, white-haired man in a black suit. He waved to them feebly. *"Hola,"* he said, the word echoing off metal, then went back into his room.

They climbed a steel ladder, the rust flaking under their hands. The rooms were offices. While they filed in, Pasquale stood aside like a doorman.

The man in the suit sat behind a desk like an executive. Apparently he was El Marichal; there was no one else. His eyes were green as a cat's and he wore an impressive gold Rolex. On the walls were topographic maps of the valley—Segovia, Arriaga, Santa Rosa. Four chairs waited for them. Pasquale stood by the door like a servant. The man nodded and he left.

"Where are the others?" Luz asked.

"Sleeping," the old man said. He spoke with only one side of his mouth, like a stroke victim. "They were busy in Segovia last night. In the morning they say there's a train."

61

"We heard," Luz said. "Pasquale says there are twelve more helicopters."

"The helicopters don't matter," the old man said, pleasing Jorge. "The men are what matter, and the weapons. We take the weapons, we win, it's that simple. The Americans can go home."

"It's impossible," Luz said. "A whole train."

"We will be careful." He turned his gaze on Jorge. "They're here for you, I suspect, *nino.*"

"Excuse me, Marichal," Luz said, "but have respect. He is the son of—"

"The son of the son of my good friend. Yes, I can see it. I call him *nino* because he's like a grandson to me, like blood. Not to make fun, never. Do you know that, *nino,* that you have the blood of a whole country in you?"

"I have known that forever," Jorge said, and though he'd only heard it just now, it was true. He'd known from the first time he'd heard his father's stories of Mariel and Galindo and San Ramos—of the Bay of Pigs, which his father would not talk about, merely spitting when anyone mentioned Kennedy.

"Whatever will happen," El Marichal said, "will happen. That is not in a man's power to change. But you are the Ortega, and many will watch you. They will tell their sons and daughters of the day the Ortega returned to Santa Rosa, whatever the outcome."

"I know," Jorge said.

"I want to make sure you know that."

"You don't have to tell me."

"I'm glad." He turned back to Luz, coolly, as if he were conducting an interview. He pointed to the empty chair. "Aurelio isn't with you."

"He had to check the radios. We only have until Monday."

"Has he become unreliable?"

"No," Luz said. "He just has the nerves. It's not the same thing."

"I understand," El Marichal said. "Please tell him I missed his company." He leaned over and opened a drawer and came up with first one and then another pair of brandy snifters. He blew the dust from them, uncorked a green bottle and poured an inch of amber fluid in each. He chose one and stood, and they all followed.

He clinked his snifter against Jorge's. "To your grandfather." He took a sip, then sat and swirled the rest around. It was hot and sweet in Jorge's throat, instantly dizzying. "But you've come for something you're having difficulty asking me, no?"

Luz looked to Jorge as if he might be in charge now. Jorge waited until she quit.

"Marichal," Luz said, "we need several men."

"Several."

"Like you needed men for the substation."

"I'm obliged, I know. It's just a difficult time. How many will you need?"

Luz looked to Jorge.

"Four," Jorge said.

"You will have them."

"And weapons," Luz said. "Light, heavy, anything you can spare."

"After the train we will have too many. You are welcome to them."

"Can we take some now?" Jorge asked.

"Tomorrow. We will need everything for the morning."

"You have recoilless rifles?"

"One. And one LAW. I will give you the men along with them, but tomorrow." He smiled and leaned back in the chair as if they were done. "Did you truly doubt me?"

"No," Luz said.

"I'm old but I never forget."

They thanked him, and the four of them sat sipping the last of the brandy. El Marichal turned to Gloria.

"And you, what have you to say? You walk fifteen miles just to sit between these two?"

"I'm supposed to listen," Gloria said. "To miss nothing."

"Why?"

"So that one day I can do this myself."

"When I'm gone," Luz explained, ignoring Jorge's look.

"Why?" El Marichal said. "Where are you going?"

"Where do you think?" Luz said. "The same place as you. Except I'll get there quicker."

"How's that?" the old man said.

"I'm taking the helicopter. You're only taking the train."

CHAPTER 11

THE MINUTE THEY STEPPED outside it began to rain, the drops dimpling the still canals. The sky was low and fast, clouds ripping themselves apart, showing their dark bellies. Pasquale had moved; he stuck his head out of the cane to wish them luck, and Jorge almost shot him.

"*Tonto!*" Lux scolded, and whacked Jorge's arm.

"It's nothing," Pasquale assured them, but Luz made Jorge apologize twice before they moved on, and then they sloshed through the mangroves without speaking, as if the whole day had gone wrong.

The canopy shielded them like a roof, the rain draining down tree trunks, streaming off leaves. Luz was still angry with him, and bulled up the hillside, leaving him breathless. The path grew slippery, their boots churning the dirt to mud. At a fork they stopped and Luz moved the clump into a corner square, showing Gloria how to change the password. Jorge wanted to ask for a sip of water, but pride stopped him. As they climbed, the air seemed thinner. Gloria kept looking back as if he were falling behind. How long had they been in these hills? Their entire lives, Jorge thought.

On top of the ridge it was pouring. The jungle gave way and suddenly they were in the clouds, the sea and the valley gone, lost beneath them. The drops were heavy, and he wished he'd worn a hat. They had to lean into the wind; it pulled tears from the corners of his eyes. The rope bridge was slippery, the monkey invisible below. Ahead, Gloria's shirt traced the bones of her shoulders, and Jorge wondered if she knew that Luz wasn't fooled, that a woman like her knew when people were lovers. It was pointless, he thought; none of them were going anywhere.

It was harder walking downhill. Twice Luz fell hard, the second time the canteen bruising her hip. She gritted her teeth and banged a fist into the mud. "Son of a whore!" They helped her up and she limped a few steps, then rested a hand on the trunk of a palm, bent over, swearing under her breath. He needed her to laugh and say it was nothing; he couldn't afford to lose her, and she knew it. But she kept spitting, hissing, blaming the world for her luck.

The rest of the way was slow. They tried to keep her off the one leg, supported her between them. It was almost dark when they came upon Teófilo crouched behind a rock, his glasses reflecting the sky's last light, giving him away. Jorge almost laughed. Teófilo saw Luz and ran out to help, his AK slung over one shoulder. He was soaked, his rolls of flab pronounced beneath his T-shirt.

"Idiot!" she swore at him. "Moron! Ask the password. We could be anybody."

He apologized, kneeling to lift her into his arms.

"Ask it!" she said, though he was already carrying her, and he did. "It's too late, you're dead and the camp is compromised."

"I saw it was you," Teófilo argued meekly.

"Useless nobody! Caterpillar!"

She kept it up until they came upon César.

"Password," he called, perfectly hidden in the brush.

"Shut up," Luz said. "I've hurt myself." Teófilo hesitated but she told him to go on.

César stepped out, wearing a poncho over his weapon. The hood's narrow bill dripped water. "I surrender command of your pack," he said, and Jorge thanked him, pleased with his loyalty.

Puddles sat atop the canvas. While the rest of them made for the cave, Jorge knelt and thumbed in the combinations and undid the straps around the trunk. He'd have to check the radio tomorrow.

Tonight he'd look at a map of the harbor and see where he needed to place his eyes. Though he hadn't really thought about it, by default he'd already decided on César and Rafael. It was a trade-off. He'd miss their guns, but there was no way Teófilo would stay alive long enough to give Jorge the information he needed. Aurelio was out. The other possibility was Hector, but he was young, and even without the do-rag, the brushburn on his nose made him stick out in a crowd. They were all unknown quantities really, but Jorge didn't have much choice. It worried him. With Luz's hip, it looked like he'd have to take the station with Hector, Teófilo, Gloria and the old man. If El Marichal came through, he'd substitute a few of his men, but that wasn't definite; they still had to do the train, and Jorge didn't think they'd succeed. He'd almost volunteered the radio and some of the plastique, then thought better of it.

Aurelio knew the radios, knew the harbor. That would free up Rafael, who'd be perfect inside the building. With himself and Gloria and the old man and Rafael, they had a chance, but that meant trusting Aurelio. He couldn't risk it.

He wondered if Forbes knew the situation he was putting him in. Probably not, he thought, hefting the pack, but then, walking down to the cave mouth, he thought that maybe that was a wish. Forbes was just far enough removed to have a clear view. Did it matter, finally? It was like the rain; it was best not to think about it, just try to get the job done.

The blanket was dark and sopping and cold on his arm when he lifted it aside. Aurelio and Francisco sat at the table, toasting each other with rum; when they saw Jorge, they turned and raised their cans, laughing. They were dry and already half bagged, Francisco's hat cockeyed. Luz lay on a bedroll by the fire, Gloria and Teófilo tending her.

"To the brave Ortega, *generalissimo* of Miami Beach!" Aurelio crowed.

"Pig," César spat at him. "Traitor."

"*Chupa ma pinga.*" Aurelio made kissing sounds at him.

"Ignore him," Luz called. "He's drunk."

César took a seat across from him. "You sit on your fat ass while we're out fighting for you."

"Fighting? Looks like you're standing out in the rain."

"You want to see fighting?"

"Shut up a minute," Jorge said, getting in between them. "Where are Felipe and the gypsy?"

Francisco looked up drunkenly from under his hat. He petted his mustache as if thinking and looked around the cave. "They're not here."

"Did you see them?"

"No," Aurelio said, refilling his glass. "They've been gone all day."

"The *viejo* should be back by now," César said.

"It's not like him," Gloria seconded.

"He probably found some little boy to play with."

"Shut up!" César slammed the table.

Aurelio laughed.

"He's drunk," Luz called again, as if to protect him.

"Hector's on guard below?" Jorge asked.

"By the main trail," César said.

Teófilo came from the back and offered to go with Jorge.

"It's easier to go alone," Jorge explained. He looked for Gloria; Luz caught his eye too. Yes, he nodded, he'd be careful.

Outside, the pool was brown, bubbles drifting across the surface, flowing over the dam. It was dusk, and he could only see the shapes of the trees. A stream surged through the ravine, then scattered on the rock ledges, making the footing treacherous. Jorge stayed down, the pistol in his fist, listening for any stray sound through the rain. Now he wished he'd asked the old man to show him a different path up from the main trail. If they'd just given him a few more days, he thought, then consciously stopped. It was a bad sign; already he was second-guessing himself.

If El Marichal could stop the train, then maybe, just maybe . . .

He reached the edge of the trail. It was mud, and he wondered about leaving footprints. He flanked the trail for a few hundred yards, then crossed backward, trying to lose his bootprints in a confusion of hooves. He came back through heavy brush, planting his feet and kneeing the high grass aside.

Ahead, above, silhouetted against the clouds, Hector perched in the crotch of a guava tree, peering down the mountain, his do-rag smooth as a bald head. Jorge gave the call of a macaw, and Hector wheeled around like a squirrel, his AK leveled at Jorge.

"What *yanqui* bird is that?"

"The sleeping bird," Jorge said. "The bird on guard duty too long."

"It's the weather," the boy said, waving a hand at the rain.

"Still, you're dead."

"Granted."

"Have you seen Felipe?"

"Hours ago. He went down with the gypsy."

"Not since."

"There's been no one, not even the evening scout. It's a night for drinking by the fire. Will we attack in this?"

"The rain's lucky," Jorge lied. "It will take Clemente's helicopters away from him."

"And our helicopters? Do we have any?"

"It will keep the streets clear."

"The traffic's bad when it rains," Hector said.

"It will take the helicopters away, that's enough. It will come down to men, as always."

"We'll have more—but only if the landing goes well. Again, it comes down to the station." Hector frowned. "How will you know to give the signal?"

"When the landing craft are ashore with their gates down."

"What if only some make it?"

"If half of them make it, I give the signal."

"That will be enough?"

"It depends on the train," Jorge admitted.

Hector was about to ask another question when they heard the swish of nylon in the dark. They both wheeled and crouched down, Jorge's wet hand on Hector's back. Someone was coming up the path, wheezing from the climb.

"Stop," Hector called and jacked the bolt back.

The shape stopped, leaving nothing but the tapping of the rain.

"Password."

"Hector is a *culo,*" Felipe said.

"Password."

"*Tiburón.*"

"You may pass, old dog's fart."

"Where have you been?" Jorge asked.

"Where you said—by the Arriaga road."

"Rafael didn't relieve you?"

"Hours ago."

"Then why didn't you come back and report? I need this information now. You know that."

"I thought it best to stay. The road's busy. It takes both of us to count everything."

"Cars?" Hector prompted.

"Not a single one," the old man said. "The *guardia* have closed the road. There are flares out, and checkpoints. I saw them pull a couple out of a Volkswagen and roll it into a field. It's all trucks pulling guns."

"Any tanks?" Jorge asked.

Felipe pulled a scrap of paper from his windbreaker and flicked his lighter. "Sixteen—so far. Rafael said he'd stay until midnight."

"I'll send someone to relieve him. Did he tell you the guard's schedule?"

"Yes," Felipe said, and dug in his pocket again. "He says there are two of them—"

"Too easy," Hector said.

"They change at seven."

"Excellent," Jorge said. It was perfect, and he needed something positive right now, something he could sell them back at the cave. "And men? Were the trucks full of them?"

"Not that I could see. It's all equipment so far."

"Good," Jorge said.

"But tanks," Hector said, stunned, and for a second he seemed the boy he was.

"We won't have to deal with them," Jorge promised. "They'll be facing the harbor." If the landing was just a diversion, he thought, it was working. He wished he could radio Forbes and let him know.

"Still," Felipe said, "they know. It will make it harder for us to move through the city."

The three fell silent, as if they understood it was pointless to speculate, especially now, a day away.

"Come, *viejo,*" Jorge said, "get some dinner. Hector, I'll send someone down to relieve you."

"*Gracias,* Ortega," the boy said, and shouldered his weapon and scaled the tree again.

Jorge led Felipe up the path. The rain was slowing down now, but still annoying, landing in his hair. At the main trail, they detoured a hundred meters east, and Felipe showed him how to point his feet up the trail, not across, so they'd blend with the hoofprints. They tromped on, using the tree trunks to pull themselves up.

Felipe stopped beside the waterfall, under a thin overhang. Water spattered off the rocks.

"You have the good cigarettes?" the old man asked, but Jorge hadn't brought any, and Felipe pulled out a brown cigarillo and lit up. It stank like burning rope. "What did El Marichal have to say?"

Jorge told him about the train, about the men he promised them.

"He's busy," Felipe said. It was an excuse, absolution, and Jorge realized he wouldn't get those men. He wanted to blame Forbes, but there was no point. By now the entire city was on alert.

"But if they stop the train," Jorge said.

"That's the only way." Felipe looked at him as if to make sure he knew it.

"Everyone forgets Forbes," Jorge said. "It's not just us. You don't know what he's bringing."

"Whatever it is," the old man said, "it will be too late to help us."

"That worries you?"

"Not me," Felipe said. "But there's nothing glorious in it either."

"You think I believe there is?"

"I suspect it. Otherwise you wouldn't be here."

Jorge wanted to pause, to digest it, but he didn't want the old man to see. "Bullshit," he said. "Now finish that. I'm hungry."

Felipe flipped the butt toward the waterfall, which batted it to the rocks.

It was fully dark in the ravine, the water higher than before, and cold on Jorge's ankles. He would have to dry everything by the fire and sleep inside tonight. It surprised him how he'd been counting on seeing Gloria, breathing the scent of her skin. It had been the same with

Catalina, the one sure thing in the middle of pure uncertainty. Was it a weakness in him, something to do with his father?

He remembered the nights in the motel—all those road trips to see spring training—listening to his father talk while they waited to fall asleep: What the ballpark was like in Santa Rosa, the sky beyond the outfield fence, the gusts of ocean wind that turned high flies into game-winning home runs, the fans with their whistles and tambourines, flinging orange peels down at the visitors' dugout—and soon Jorge would be dreaming of that country he'd never seen, and his grandfather's fabled death (never mentioned) at the Bay of Pigs, and then his mother, and finally nothing at all but the long fall into soft darkness, comforted by the knowledge that tomorrow they'd eat the ninety-nine-cent breakfast and see the White Sox and Pirates and then the Reds and Yankees later before they came back and lay down again and Jorge said, "Tell me about the old times."

All that was gone, along with the BarcaLounger and the TV, *The Game of the Week,* the big Lincoln his father washed in the driveway every Saturday morning, his mother's closet full of bright, perfumed dresses. He was here, now, following the old man across the pool. He had to be sharper, he thought, and concentrated on the voice above, leaking through the blanket. Even muffled, it sounded like shouting. Instinctively, his hand went for the pistol, though he knew it was probably just Aurelio, sloppy drunk. As they climbed the wet stairs, a woman screamed, and Jorge ran for the blanket.

It was bright inside, and warm. The first thing he saw was Aurelio on the floor, and César above him, kicking him in the face. Luz was screaming, Gloria and Francisco trying to tear him away. César threw another kick, but his boot skipped off Aurelio's forehead, leaving a black streak of polish. Aurelio was out, his teeth bleeding into his beard. César's arm was cut, his sleeve sopping red. "Son of a bitch!" he screamed. "I'll kill you!"

"Hold on!" Jorge showed him the pistol, holding it high, the barrel pointed toward the ceiling. He straight-armed César away from Aurelio and stood above the downed man. Felipe stayed at his arm like a partner. In the back, Luz was sobbing.

"Kill him!" César screamed. He had scratches on his forehead, and he was gasping, his neck sweaty.

"Shut up," Jorge said.

"He provokes me, the coward. He lies and curses you."

"He's drunk," Luz cried.

"He had a knife," Gloria said, and pointed to it on the floor.

"What's this about?" Jorge asked. He still had the gun up, as if they might attack him.

"He insulted you," César said, clutching his bloody sleeve. "He said you slept with Gloria."

"For this you kill him?"

"It's a lie and an insult to her honor."

Jorge waited for someone else to speak, but no one did. At his feet, Aurelio moaned.

"It's not a lie," Jorge said.

"It's still an insult. It's an insult for you to say it."

"It's no insult to me," Gloria said.

"Then you are without honor," César said. He looked to Jorge as if to challenge him, then shook off Francisco and bolted out of the cave, the blanket swinging back.

"Go after him," Jorge ordered Felipe.

"Where will he go?" the old man said, and Jorge gave up.

"I couldn't stop them," Gloria apologized.

"He has a big mouth," Felipe explained.

Francisco shrugged and clapped his hat back on and sat down to his rum as if it were nothing, just some barroom dust-up.

Aurelio moaned and lolled his head to one side. The blood shone on his lips. With his scars and the beard, it was hard to tell how badly he was hurt. Gloria fetched a bedroll and they lifted him on it and carried him back toward the fire.

In his head, Jorge totaled up the damage. Aurelio was even more likely to turn against them. He'd been counting on César; now he couldn't trust him. On top of that, it had been César's right arm. Luz with her hip. Just bad luck. He looked to his watch, but it was gone.

Luz was still sobbing. "He was drunk," she cried. "He was drunk."

CHAPTER 12

THE FIRE HISSED FROM the rain spitting down the chimney. Rafael sat before it on a plastic bucket with his shirt off, shaking a bottle of hot sauce over a bowl of rice. Luz lay on one side of him, awake, Aurelio on the other, still moaning incoherently. The blood had come off but the shoe polish lingered, a dark comet like a bruise across his forehead. Jorge ordered Francisco to go sober up and replace Hector on watch. César hadn't come back yet.

"It makes things difficult," Rafael said. He pointed his fork at Aurelio. "I trust this one even less."

"It's nothing," Luz shrugged. "It's inevitable, those two, just bad timing."

"No," Felipe said. "You know him. He'll go after César."

Luz said nothing.

"You should have killed him the other night," Rafael said, turning to Jorge and Gloria.

"He's been good," Luz protested. "There's no need."

Felipe disagreed. He was smoking one of his stinking cigarillos.

"Let's take a vote," Rafael said. "César and myself are for it."

"No one's voting for anything," Jorge said. He and Gloria had been

73

playing gin, and now he threw down his cards and stood. "He was drunk. I'm not going to kill him for being drunk."

"We'll have to watch him all the time," Felipe said, and it hurt Jorge that the old man was against him. The professor had never challenged him; it was only Catalina. "Who will do it? We don't have enough men."

"I'll do it," Luz said.

"You can barely walk."

"I will," Gloria said.

"Pah," Rafael scoffed.

"Hector will," Jorge said. "Right now we need everybody, even him."

"Thank you," Aurelio croaked, and they all turned to him, lying by the fire. His eyes were open but he didn't move. "Even me. That's very kind." He spoke thickly, as if immensely tired, punch-drunk.

Jorge went over to him and knelt down.

"Ortega, such a passionate defense. I didn't know you loved me."

"I don't."

"More than these jackals." He tried to spit in Rafael's direction, but the bloody phlegm fell on his chin. "Tell them I am with you now."

"Are you?"

"I am here," Aurelio said. "That's enough."

It proved nothing to Jorge, but he let it go. No one spoke, as if they were ashamed. The silence was just, he thought; they'd earned it.

Gloria helped Luz over to Aurelio and Jorge laid her bedroll on the floor so they could be together. Rafael and Felipe retreated to the table; Jorge and Gloria joined them and resumed playing. What more could possibly go wrong, he thought, then checked himself. He would be thankful now for the quiet. He knew he wouldn't sleep tonight. He picked up a jack and got rid of a three. The rain fell. The fire hissed.

THE RAIN STOPPED around five and the wind lashed the trees. The noise woke Jorge. He was surprised he could sleep. Beside him, Gloria dreamed, her face bathed radium-green by the dial of his watch, her eyes sliding beneath her lids. For an instant she seemed a stranger, some pickup down on South Beach—a rollerblader in a funky leotard, a swimsuit model stopping by the tiers of cheap sunglasses—and he was ashamed. It was true though, he didn't know her at all, and he wondered if in all his life he was meant to know only Catalina.

He saw the double ruts of the service road beneath the power lines, the dust kicked up by the professor's burro, then shook it out of his head. Why not his father? It couldn't torture him more.

He slipped his legs from under the bedroll and stood. The stone was cold, in back the fire dying. Luz and Aurelio hadn't moved; César was still missing. Jorge felt his way along the wall until his hand touched the wet blanket. He pulled it back and the warm wind made him squint.

Outside, through the canopy, the sky was coloring to the east, cloudless, the stars brilliant. It was a gift, and Jorge stood there transfixed, appreciating it. It would help El Marichal as well. He couldn't stop himself from imagining how it would all fall into place—the train, the extra men, the weapons. He was lost in this reverie when César called to him from the stairs.

"Ortega," he whispered, and Jorge had to cast around to find him. "Over here."

He was wedged into a niche in the wall, sitting up in his bedroll, his weapon at the ready.

Jorge came down the stairs in his undershirt. "I knew you wouldn't leave us."

"It's not out of love," César said. "Where would I go?"

"I'm happy you're staying."

"Who's afraid of a coward?"

"I'm sorry if I insulted you," Jorge said. He didn't want to say her name.

"Only the heart is offended," César said. "It's a weak muscle in me, I fear. I can't help but hold it against you—and her—though there's no reason. She'd only hurt me. It doesn't make sense."

"I'm sorry."

"Don't waste your pity. I wouldn't if I could help it. But sometimes there's no helping it."

"I know," Jorge said, because he did. They faced each other in the dim light, but there was nothing more to say, so they turned and looked up through the canopy. Typical island weather, he thought; there was no guarantee it would be like this tomorrow.

"Go," César said. "She's waiting for you."

"I'm glad you're back."

"Don't make love to me, your heart isn't in it. Now go."

Lifting the blanket, Jorge looked back, but he could barely see him, just a dark seam in the rock.

Gloria muttered as he slipped in, then settled, a warm leg thrown over him. Her hair smelled of the fire and Felipe's cigarillos, and he kissed her on her part. He felt selfish, being awake, not dreaming along with her. He tilted his wrist to check his watch again. Twenty-six hours. There was too much to do, yet he wished he could sleep, forget all this, wake in the morning to find Gloria on the balcony in his Marlins jersey, watching the joggers chug up and down the beach.

He closed his eyes, and there was Catalina slapping her burro on the rump, the three wires dipping high above them, rising to meet the insulators of the next standard. The professor was wearing his ridiculous bush hat with the one side pinned up like some Aussie in a World War II movie. Catalina glanced back at Jorge and stuck out her tongue. He had the plastique in his saddle bag, enough to not quite take down one tower. His orders were to make it look like the work of an amateur, which he supposedly was—a Honduran Army deserter, a sympathizer. The rebels were supposed to be gaining strength, the capital at risk, plunged into darkness, chaos. The entire thing was a lie, a ruse to spin the elections the next month, to nail down another year of military funding from the State Department. It was what the Company paid him for, to fix things. He stuck his tongue out at Catalina and she smiled. The burros nodded, plodding along.

He rolled over and Gloria stirred, protesting. He brought his watch up and tipped the dial so he could see her face. Heavy black brows, a saddle of freckles over her nose. Could she betray him? Of course. It was easy. He wasn't dumb enough to trust her.

Paranoid, he thought. Stop it.

He nestled against her, smelled the salty heat of her rising between them, the day's hike over the mountains a subtle musk on her skin. It pleased him, but now that he remembered the power lines, he could not get the possibilities out of his head. The tattoo from the *federale* was no comfort; they were easily faked. The teeth weren't beyond a dentist, the broken nose a well-thrown punch.

He recognized that he was projecting and stopped himself. Everything was fine. He wasn't lying this time. He liked this better, being on the right side. It meant less cover, and a cleaner feeling afterward. That was why the Company made sure to move you around, gave you a plush job after a bad one. Losing was too hard. Like surviving.

HE WOKE TO GUNFIRE, instinctively rolling away from the commotion. It came from outside, the quick clanking burst of an automatic. He grabbed at his pack, then remembered the pistol was under the edge of the bedroll.

"Here," Gloria said, shoving the grip at him.

Rafael beat Jorge outside. The flap swung back and scratched his nose.

In the pool floated a cavalry officer, facedown in his gray cape. The water was muddy, churned up. César stood on the stairs above him, breathing hard, still covering the man with his M-16. There was no motion in the limbs. Rafael leveled the Mac-10 at him as if he were faking. One boot had fallen off, revealing a red sock with a hole in the heel. Beyond the dam a dappled gelding wandered in the ravine, his reins trailing in the water. The officer turned with the current, his hat drifting just out of reach of his gloved hand.

"The son of a bitch," Rafael said. "How'd he get here?"

"I don't care," Jorge said. "We've got to get rid of him."

Aurelio and Felipe were there, and Hector and Gloria; the only one still inside was Luz. Felipe had his boots on and his windbreaker over his underwear. His legs were gray, his knees lumpy. He waded down the ravine after the horse, cooing, trying not to spook him. They all watched, silent. The big gelding stopped, skittish, nickering and twitching his ears. The old man drew even with him and stroked his neck. He wrapped the reins around his fist and stood there, whispering to him.

The officer's hat tumbled over the dam and headed for the ravine, bobbing. No one made a move to stop the body. It ran aground, one arm reaching over the dam.

"We bury him here," Aurelio ordered, pointing above the cave. Jorge was surprised by how forceful he sounded, as if the beating had restored his senses, his pride. "I'll take the horse around the mountain. Who's on guard below?"

"Francisco," Hector said.

"He's either dead or asleep. I don't care which. How many times did you fire?"

"Only once," César said. "On semiautomatic."

"Good. Go down to the waterfall with Rafael. If he's just the morning scout, we're all right."

"What if he's not?" César asked.

"We're screwed," Aurelio said, and the two threw their boots on and took off splashing down the ravine. The gelding shied sideways, and Felipe hauled on the reins, cursing.

"I can ride him," Hector offered.

"No," Aurelio said. "It's the one thing I can do." He looked to Jorge as if for permission. His face was puffy from last night, one eye almost closed. "If it's a patrol, I'll take them around the mountain."

Jorge looked to Gloria, then to Hector. They didn't say anything. Aurelio seemed to understand.

"Go," Jorge said, and Aurelio smiled and whacked him on the shoulder and dashed inside to get dressed. Hector followed him in.

"What are you doing?" Gloria said. "You think he's with us now?"

"I'd rather find out now than tomorrow."

"He probably turned us in himself."

"He wouldn't do that," Jorge said. "He's just afraid of the station."

"How can you say that? You don't know him at all."

"I know him as well as I know you."

79

"That's what I just said. You don't know him."

Aurelio came out with an old carbine holstered low on his thigh. "Don't fight over me. I won't disappoint you."

"I know that, Don Aurelio."

"Take care of Luz. I'll be back by nightfall."

He clopped down the stairs, Gloria scowling after him. He waded across the stream below the dam where the officer lay, then bent over and untied his wet cape, wrung it out and threw it over his shoulders. He fished the hat out and knocked it against his leg and fit it on. Felipe held the gelding steady for him, and he climbed on and trotted off down the ravine.

"I don't like it," Gloria said.

"What can he tell them?" Jorge said. "They know everything already."

"Still," she said, but didn't go on.

Below, Felipe was struggling with the body, trying to lift it free of the dam. They went down to help him.

The officer was no bigger than Francisco. When they pulled him out of the water, they saw where César had hit him—just under the heart. He must have stuck six rounds in him; there was a hole in his ribs the size of a cereal bowl. Jorge got him under one arm, Felipe the other, and they dragged him up the stairs between them like a drunk. Gloria came behind them with the missing boot, swearing at the man for being such a nuisance. There was mud in his hair, and when they laid him down, brown water ran out of his mouth. He had a shiny .45 and a pair of bandoliers crossed on his chest; the rifle was probably still with the horse. Felipe knelt and went through his pockets, rolling him over.

Jorge turned and peered down the ravine. So far they hadn't heard gunshots; it was a good sign. Aurelio would have reached the main trail by now, if he was taking that way.

"He's one of Clemente's," Felipe said, handing him a military ID. Jorge immediately forgot the name, erased the face in the picture. Felipe gave him a wallet shot of a family—the man in a suit with his wife and two girls in pigtails.

"Put them back," he said. "We'll bury him with them."

Hector was happy to stay in the cave and watch Luz and Jorge's pack.

"An officer," Luz said. "Good." She spat in the fire.

Gloria told her about Aurelio.

"Are you worried?" Luz asked.

"Not me," Jorge said, and she looked to Gloria.

"It's my influence," Luz said. "I've taught you not to trust him."

"For good reasons," Gloria said.

"There's no time to argue," Luz said, and shooed them.

The officer lay in a puddle on the rocks. Jorge lifted him under his arms, Felipe by his ankles. For such a small man, he was heavy. It was probably all the water. Gloria walked ahead of them with the boot, looking for a good spot. It was fully day now, the air under the canopy beginning to warm. It wouldn't take long for the body to rot. As they made their way up the hillside, he couldn't keep his eyes off the man's sock. A vision of the professor and Catalina in the bed of the pickup flashed before him—their bare feet poking out of the plastic, red clay between their toes, clumps stuck to their blue ankles.

Jorge bit his lip to bring himself back. The dead man's head butted his stomach. His eyes were open, already clouding over, and with every step he nodded and his teeth clicked together.

Gloria froze—crouched down, a hand silently flung behind her to stop them. She cocked her head and listened like a hunter, her eyes sliding from side to side.

The leaves above rustled, tapped at each other, and then from far off, steadily, like the monotonous song of some mechanical insect, came the nattering of a helicopter. Jorge hoped it was just one, then just two. Several more joined the chorus.

Though there was no point, he and Felipe slipped into the brush, covering the officer with their bodies. Still distant, the choppers thumped the air, the rotors' echoes caroming down the valley. Jorge didn't have to see their stubby profiles to know they were the same squadron of Werewolves from the other day. He wondered if they did have infrared. Their cannon could shred the entire hillside, leave nothing but smoking tree trunks and burnt earth. He hoped Aurelio could hear them.

The first wave came over in the same diamond formation. Felipe said something but the noise was too much. Jorge waited for them to break and bank around and angle in for a strafing run. They kept formation, stayed straight, headed north, inland.

"They're not for us," the old man shouted.

"No," he agreed.

Gloria scuttled over. "Arriaga." She pointed, and Jorge remembered the train.

"El Marichal," he said, just as another four came over, deafening them. He wasn't sure they'd heard, but from their silence as they watched the diamond fly over, the long pause before they turned in unison toward the next four, he saw that it didn't matter. They knew.

CHAPTER 15

THEY SHOVED THE OFFICER'S boot into his tunic and buried him standing up in a gap in a creek bank, walling him in with handfuls of mud. Gloria did his face, grimacing. The rains would discover him later; all they needed was a day.

Luz agreed they would have to abandon the cave after tomorrow.

"Maybe we won't need it," she tried, but no one believed it. Gloria looked at her hip; the bone was ringed with purple, a yellow halo. It hurt her to walk. Probably just a pointer, Jorge thought; he'd seen bunches on Parris Island, after the obstacle course. In a week she'd be fine, but that didn't help them now. They had no way of moving her.

Hector returned with Francisco, who was weaponless and missing his hat, blood from a cut under one eye seeping into his mustache. Hector kept a pistol in his back as if he were a prisoner. He motioned for Francisco to sit at the table, pressed the muzzle against his neck.

"What are you doing?" Felipe scolded, pushing the gun away.

Hector holstered it. "He admits he fell asleep."

"So he fell asleep," Luz said. "This isn't the *guardia.*"

"It's my fault," Francisco said. "I accept my punishment."

"Shut up," Hector ordered, and Francisco cringed.

Gloria stepped between them. "How do you know he came in that way?"

"You can see the tracks. They went right by him."

"Is this true?" Luz said.

Francisco looked to Hector first. "It's true."

"See? He admits it."

"So what?" Gloria said. "You've never fallen asleep on guard?"

"I never let the cavalry past me."

"That's not what I asked." She stayed in his face, hands on her hips.

"Ortega," Hector appealed.

"An apology is all that's necessary," Jorge said.

Francisco turned to Luz. "I beg your forgiveness, *comandante.*"

"You will do better," Luz said.

"I promise with all my heart."

"That's it?" Hector cried.

"No," Jorge said. "Now you, apologize to him."

"For what—teaching him his duty?"

"For not treating him like a brother."

Hector spat. "He is no brother to me."

"Go then," Jorge said. "We don't need you."

"He fell asleep on guard!" Hector pleaded.

"That's done with, that's nothing. Tomorrow is everything. Apologize."

Hector said it without looking at Francisco.

"This is acceptable to you?" Jorge asked. He kept his eyes on Francisco's to let him know it wasn't a question.

"I would apologize to Hector as well."

Hector said nothing until Gloria pushed him in the back.

"Don't be stupid," Jorge said. "We need to be together. Tonight no one drinks."

"Yes, Don Jorge," Francisco said.

Jorge was about to send them down to spell Rafael and César when he heard a muffled explosion. For a moment they all froze, then grabbed their weapons and ran outside, Jorge in the lead.

He didn't see anything and crept down the stairs, his back against the rock wall. The dam burbled, and then from above came a series of thuds like mortars hitting home—but soft, in the distance, though it still made them duck.

"The train," Felipe said.

"Stay with Luz," Jorge ordered him, and led the rest up the path. As they climbed, the crashing seemed closer, each report making him blink. Teófilo wasn't at his post—probably scared off, Jorge guessed, or hiding in some thicket. Far off, Werewolves chopped the air. Jorge wondered how many Clemente had sent. He thought of El Marichal in his beautiful suit, his graciousness. Already he was getting sentimental; it was just intuition, the habit of bad luck.

They came out of the jungle into bright sunlight, the leaves gleaming as if waxed. It wasn't far to the ridge, and he shouldered his sixteen and began to run. Though his throat burned, he thought he was getting used to the air. The trail leveled off and the dirt gave way to granite, slippery and unforgiving beneath his boots.

"Here," Gloria said, and cut in front of him, her hair flying behind. They followed her through a confusion of boulders until they were perched on a bald outcrop overlooking the valley.

A fire burned along the river, by the rail line, the wind combing the smoke toward Arriaga. A knot of Werewolves flitted around the dark column, pouring rockets and cannon into the fields. On the tracks sat the black line of a train. At this distance, Jorge couldn't tell if it was burning or if that was just the sugar. It wasn't moving. They'd probably mined the tracks, then let loose on the survivors and taken off before the choppers could respond, leaving a rear guard to cover their retreat. He hoped so.

"They've done it!" Gloria pointed.

"They've stopped it at least," Jorge said. "Who's got binoculars?"

No one did. He told Francisco to run down and get his field glasses from Felipe.

They stood there and watched the smoke, the flashes as rockets detonated in the cane.

"They have too many helicopters," Hector said.

"It won't help them in the city," Gloria reminded him. It surprised Jorge. She was just echoing what he'd said—the logic was solid—yet, hearing it from someone else's mouth, he didn't believe it.

"It won't hurt them," Hector said. "The harbor's wide open, like a field."

"We'll have our own by then," Jorge said, though there was no guarantee. If the landing was just a diversion, they wouldn't waste them. Maybe some old Sea Kings, a few Hueys, but nothing serious. The age and the sheer number of them would tell him if Forbes meant business. "They won't be a factor."

A plume of fire bloomed, a second later a faint pop reaching them. "They're a factor now," Hector said.

The Werewolves circled and nosed over and dove, shot their rockets and pulled up and came around again. Jorge watched Gloria and Hector watching them. It was their first time, and they couldn't look away, stood mesmerized like kids watching a magician. He'd seen enough of it to know the show meant nothing. It was pretty, true, but what mattered could only be tallied after the smoke cleared. He needed ten able bodies to take the station; right now he had nine, and that included Aurelio. He had five automatic rifles when he needed eight. To do the retreat seriously he needed the LAW El Marichal had promised. While the Werewolves were spectacular, it still came down to numbers—and really, the will to look beyond them and carry out the mission anyway. To get the job done, as his father would say.

His father had taught him that, certainly. On the TV table he'd laid out his papers beside his empty can of Bud—his retirement package, the deed to the house, the Town Car's title already signed over to Jorge. He'd even covered them with a sheet of Saran wrap, neat as a hospital meal. When the detective showed it to him, Jorge stood looking at it a minute, imagined how pleasing those last preparations must have been for him. Everything in order, everything settled. "Thanks," he said.

Another pillar of flame spiked to the sky, and Gloria swore and stepped toward the edge, as if to go after them. Jorge took her arm but she jerked it away. "Bastard Fidelistas!" She spat in their direction, the white glob plummeting over the edge. She swore till she had to catch her breath.

"Tomorrow," she said passionately, "we'll massacre them."

"Maybe," Jorge said.

"Definitely."

"Ho," Hector called, "here's the useless one," and Francisco clambered through the rocks, gasping. He handed the case over and Jorge pulled out the glasses. He flicked the switch and they hummed and he lifted them to his eyes.

The picture was fuzzy, and he thumbed the rangefinder until the smoke came into focus, roiling up oilily.

"What do you see?" Gloria asked.

The Werewolves were paired up, turning with rigid precision. One set nosed over and sent their rockets smoking into the cane. The fireball filled his vision, then subsided, revealing the train in the background.

It was still on the tracks, its windows covered with riveted sheets of armor, one of which bore a ragged gash—the mark of El Marichal's LAW. It appeared they'd only fired once. Tracers blazed from neatly spaced slits. He'd seen the same train in El Salvador, the gunports' fields of fire completely engineered, the doors sealed off. The one down there had had skulls instead of running lamps to intimidate the peasants.

"What is it?" she asked.

"The train."

He followed the tracers into the maze of canals. He didn't see anyone returning fire. The cane was burning. He caught a glimpse of a body floating, another collapsed half on the bank.

"Is it burning?"

"The cane is."

"Do you see El Marichal?"

"I see a few of his men," he said, but now it was more than a few bodies scattered through the fields. They drifted in the canals, lay charred among the stubble. He stopped and held on one, a heavy man with a goatee and hip sunglasses—Pasquale.

He shifted the glasses to the front of the train and the world blurred.

They'd tried to stop it at a crossing. The nose of the engine was buried in a clutter of burning trucks, flames licking the windows, their tires still on fire, chuffing out clouds. El Marichal had hoped to take the train by surprise, hit it quick and get out before Clemente scrambled air support. It was stupid, Jorge thought; he could have given him enough plastique to derail it, flip the damn thing on its roof *and* rip up the track so the next one couldn't get through. This didn't do anything except lose him the men and the weapons Jorge needed. They should have talked, gone over it. Jorge should have helped him.

"Did they do it?" Hector asked.

"Yes," Jorge said, and handed the glasses to Gloria.

"Ha, the old *maricón,* I knew he could!"

"Let me see," Francisco said, but Gloria fended him off.

"They're just shooting from the train." She looked to Jorge as if this were wrong, and Francisco snatched the glasses.

"The old man surprised them," Jorge explained. "They decided it was better to wait for support."

"What kind of train is that?"

"Fortified," Francisco said, and handed the glasses to Hector. "I've heard of them, but this is the first one I've ever seen."

"Madre de Dios," Hector said. "What a mess. There's Ernesto, the poor bastard. And that looks like Tomás by the bridge there. Why are they still firing? They're all dead."

"That's good," Jorge insisted.

"That's good?" Hector asked.

"Every minute they stay there helps us." He took back the glasses. The Werewolves nosed over for another run. There was no movement in the cane, only the spray of mud thrown up, the flames. The train's gunports blazed.

"How many men does El Marichal have?" he asked.

"Twenty-five," Gloria guessed.

"Less," Hector said.

Jorge came up with sixteen, and there was a white lump in a canal that might have been another. With the smoke he couldn't see everything.

He handed the glasses to Francisco. "Watch them. When it stops, come down and tell us. And don't let the helicopters see you."

Gloria led them through the rocks again. Jorge stayed behind her, trying to use the time to think. It was so close now. There really wasn't much he could do. Get them ready. Pick the right person for each job. Check the equipment.

Behind them in the valley, heavy automatics crackled, the Werewolves thumped the air. Vacation was over, he thought. Time to go to work.

"SO," LUZ ASKED, "how did it go?" She sat upright by the fire, pressing a stinking poultice against her hip. Felipe was stirring some sort of porridge in the black pot, dripping raw cane syrup into it. The tinny radio was going. Jorge thought maybe Teófilo would be there, but he wasn't.

"It went well," Jorge said.

Hector said nothing.

"Gloria says the train was fortified."

"Yes."

"How many cars?"

"Maybe ten," he said, though in truth he'd forgotten to count them.

"Lots of helicopters."

Jorge agreed to this too.

"Still, it went well?"

"They're holding the train there."

"He's a good man, El Marichal, the last of the old *comandantes*. Tonight you should ask him about your grandfather. He has stories."

"Have you seen Teófilo?" Jorge asked, evading the issue completely. Again, Hector said nothing, and Jorge counted it in his favor. He wondered if he could trust him as he could César and Rafael. He'd need one of them inside the building.

"Not this morning," Luz said.

"He wasn't up there."

"Strange."

"Maybe he was hiding," Hector said. "Or sleeping."

"Maybe he ran off," Felipe said. "Or turned himself in."

"Not Teófilo," Gloria said.

"Then where is he?"

"Not at his post," Jorge said, and looked around the cave so everyone could see he was disappointed. He held one finger up, the way his father did when he was lecturing him. "It's the wrong time to get sloppy. Tomorrow when it's all done, then we can screw around. Right now we've got to be sharper." He punctuated the speech by leaving—another trick of his father's.

Outside it was warmer. The Werewolves still chittered in the distance. He unslung his rifle and bounded down the stairs two at a time. He stepped over the dam and moved through the ravine quietly, careful not to splash. The stream was cool on his boots, the bottom soft, and he wanted to think all the blood from the officer was long gone. He wondered if El Marichal had been with his men or whether right now he was waiting for them in the silence of the mill, sitting at his desk with a cigar and a snifter of brandy.

It was stupid. They should have just blown the tracks. There were any number of antitank mines that could have done it. They were cheap, even. In El Salvador teenagers sold them by the roadside like hubcaps. It was typical; for want of a hundred-dollar land mine, the country was lost. He pictured himself at a thousand-dollar-a-plate fund-raiser in Miami, holding up just such a device, asking the patrons to take out their checkbooks for the cause. Idiots. If they really wanted to do something, they'd have stayed here, not run off with their suitcases stuffed with money.

The image was his mother's. She was fond of telling Jorge how his father had brought nothing but one set of clothes, the rest of the bag fat with worthless pesos. How she laughed at that. Then she went dead serious. They worked the sugar camps, slept in concrete block barracks filled with rats. Before he was born. Oh, he didn't know what that man had put her through. Every night, she said, she scrubbed his underwear in the sinks. She held her hands up like a surgeon, as if they were still filthy with him.

He caught himself splashing, and slowed, concentrating on each step. The ravine gave way to sunlight, and the stream dissipated over a great shale ledge, dripping into the lush jungle. Below, the path to the waterfall was empty. It was steep, and Jorge strapped his rifle across his back and wiped his feet before going down sideways, braking and sliding, loosing a scree of pebbles. That officer must have been one hell of a rider, he thought. Aurelio too. He wondered if he could be trusted again. It was nervousness, all this thinking. He almost fell, and caught himself. At the bottom, he popped the safety off his sixteen and clicked the selector to semiautomatic. Ahead, around the bend, the falls spattered on the rocks, distracting him. He kept to the shadows, one shoulder brushing the vines that webbed the stone wall.

César and Rafael lay on the far side of the waterfall, rifles trained on the main trail below. As Jorge ducked under the falls, Rafael looked back and held up a hand as if there were danger. Jorge stopped.

Rafael waved him over. Jorge stayed low, then lay flat beside him. César pointed down at the trail.

A cavalry patrol was passing, fanned out and scanning the jungle. Looking for their friend, Jorge thought. Six, maybe seven—the leaves shielded them. They all wore the same gray hat and cape. Jorge didn't see a radio. Automatically he raised his sight to the chest of the lead horseman, kept the bead steady on his heart.

"Wait until they move into the open up here," Rafael whispered.

"We'll have to get all of them," Jorge said.

"We will."

"No."

A fly lighted on Jorge's forearm. He flexed the muscle but it didn't flinch. He blew on it. The patrol was drawing even with them, their profiles thin—harder targets. The fly bit him and took off again.

"We've got them," Rafael begged.

"The odds are bad."

"There are three of us," César argued.

"Think," Jorge said. "If one escapes, that's it—poof."

The leader passed behind a tree, and Jorge tracked him, picked him up on the other side. He had him high in the back, just under the left shoulder blade.

"I can get the first two," Rafael said.

"The first two aren't the problem. It's all of them—*and* the horses. That's fourteen."

"We can't just let them go."

"Any other day, I'd say fine."

"It's cowardly," César said.

"Say that again?"

"Excuse me, Don Jorge, but—"

"But nothing. We can't get the horses. Can *you* get the horses?" He checked their faces, making sure, then let the leader walk out of his sights and lowered his weapon.

Rafael followed, then César, with a grimace. They watched silently as the patrol passed, swallowed up by the jungle.

"It makes me sick," Rafael said. "We'll only have to kill them again."

"I know that," Jorge said, "but after tomorrow we'll have help."

"You really believe that?" Rafael said.

"I don't have a choice."

"And us?" César said. "What choice do we have?"

"I can't answer that," Jorge said.

"What happened with El Marichal?" César asked.

Jorge told them it was mostly a success.

"A very loud success," Rafael said. "I wish Aurelio such a success. So, what is left to do?"

"I need you to go down to the road again." He thought of giving him the plastique, but there wasn't enough to take out a bridge. At best it would make a crater. "You'll have to leave your rifle."

"I can't use it anyway," Rafael complained, and handed it to him. "What am I counting now?"

"Everything, but especially men—and tanks, anything armored. Come back at nightfall. César, you stay here in case the cavalry comes back. And no shooting unless you absolutely have to."

He gave Rafael his pistol and told them both to be careful. Climbing back up toward the ravine, Jorge thought that he was responsible for everything, that they were his men now. He was unsure how he felt about it. He was proud of them, but for the wrong reasons. They were trying to pull off the impossible. And while he knew it was romantic and finally juvenile, he couldn't help but admire that one quality he himself lacked: they were not afraid to die.

CHAPTER **17**

FRANCISCO CAME BACK as they were finishing lunch. He gave Jorge the glasses without a word and sat down, took off his straw cowboy hat and wiped his brow with the back of his arm. He seemed pale and dull, hungover, drawn from sleeplessness. The cut under his eye still glistened.

"It's all over?" Jorge asked.

He nodded. "The helicopters are gone."

"And the train?"

"In Arriaga by now. They took the bodies. The fields are burning, but there's nothing there."

"You haven't seen Teófilo," Luz asked.

"No."

Felipe brought him a plate of beans and tortillas. Francisco looked at it, then lit a cigarette. He put a hand to his forehead, shielding his eyes, and absently tapped the ash into the food.

"That was good food," Gloria scolded, and he pushed the plate away and covered his eyes again. When he was finished with the cigarette, he lit another. No one spoke.

"What is it?" Jorge asked.

He didn't answer, dabbed a thumb at the corner of his mustache as if he were thinking. Hector shrugged at Jorge.

"They didn't take all of the bodies," Francisco finally said. He didn't look at anybody, kept his hand over his eyes, taking a deep drag. "They lined them up beside the train. One man held them while another chopped their hands and feet off with a pair of bolt cutters. Then the man holding them stood up and put one foot on the chest and they cut off the head. Then they made a pile and poured gas on it and burned what was left."

"Bastards!" Gloria spat.

It was not new to Jorge; in El Salvador they did it to ID the rebels and piss off the families of the victims. He tried to appear shocked along with everyone else. It was war; what did they expect? He could see the stumps of Catalina's fingers. They'd taken them knuckle by knuckle to get everything out of her, even though they knew it already. Another game they played. The professor wasn't wearing pants; he had a black dusting of electrical burns running up his inseam, a nib of bright copper wire still stuck in his dark skin like a splinter.

"How many dead?" Luz asked.

"Twenty. More. I didn't count them."

"You always count," Luz said. "Everybody, remember: you always count. Was El Marichal with them?"

"I couldn't tell. They put the heads in a burlap sack and the hands and feet in another. It took both men to lift them up the stairs." He laughed. "They fell one time, and the fat one yelled at the skinny one. See, there was a fat one and a skinny one, like in a cartoon, and the fat one—"

"Enough," Luz said.

"Wait, wait," he said, and laughed, barely catching his breath, as if he were telling a hilarious joke. "The fat one had the bag on top of him."

"Enough, I said."

"He was screaming—aaahhh, help me!" Francisco couldn't stop laughing.

"Shut up!" she said, but still he giggled, and Jorge made Hector take him outside.

"Twenty is not a success," Luz said. "Twenty is a massacre. And the train's in Arriaga. That's an outright failure."

"They still have to get here," Jorge said.

"Who's going to stop them? We can't—we don't have enough people. We don't have enough people to take your station. Do all of you understand that? We don't have enough people to take the station."

"We do," Jorge insisted. It was pointless; even if they weren't operating under radio silence, he couldn't call the landing off. Again he wondered if it was just a diversion, something to draw the bulk of their Werewolves south.

"How many do you need—ten? We have seven."

"Nine," Jorge said.

"You're including me, and I can barely walk. Teófilo's gone back to the farm. That's seven to do the job of ten."

"You sound like Aurelio," Gloria said.

"Why argue?" Felipe said. "Seven or nine, it's got to be done."

"Granted," Luz said. "I'm just saying it will be difficult."

"We've known that from the beginning," Gloria said.

"It's different now," Luz said.

Jorge agreed, surprising them. "But the *viejo* is right, it's got to be done."

"Even if it *can't* be done," Luz challenged him.

"Yes," Jorge said. "Even then."

"Well, that's proof," she said. "You really are an *americano.*"

CHAPTER 18

JORGE CLEARED OFF the cards and the tuna can they used for an ash-tray and spread the acetate map on the table. He weighted the corners with clips from his sixteen so the downtown was smooth and fished a grease pencil from his pack. Luz sat at his side; Felipe and Gloria leaned over the streets. He'd sent Hector to stand guard above and Francisco below to help César by the waterfall. Aurelio and Teófilo still hadn't come back, and the afternoon was dwindling, though no one mentioned these facts. Even Luz seemed to have given up on El Marichal.

Jorge worked backward from the station, drawing a fat black line through the park, then turned left into the *mercado*. Luz had that part figured out. They'd pretend to be farmers hauling to market. Felipe's nephew drove for a government collective and had access to an old flatbed. They'd pack the truck with empty melon crates, arrange a few full ones on top for camouflage, throw a canvas over it and ride in underneath them. There was an abandoned building next to the *mercado* they could back into. After that, she had fake papers for all of them except Jorge, who could still pass as Diego Vargas. It was only two blocks to the park.

"Except for the ones who will be your eyes," Gloria corrected her, leaning over and reaching a finger toward the harbor. "They've got to make it here."

"*With* the radios," Felipe said.

"Who have you chosen?" Luz asked.

"Rafael and César." Jorge expected praise for this decision, but no one said anything. It was obvious: they were the strongest, the smartest—naturally the first to be sacrificed.

"They can't take rifles," Luz said. "They'll be stopped."

"Pistols only. They'll be dressed as vendors with packs full of breadfruit."

"By the harbor?"

"No one will notice."

"*Ay,*" Luz said, "you are wishful."

"I'll have them here"—he pointed to the tips of the jetties—"and here."

"Not so far out," Felipe offered. "They'll need some kind of cover."

"These beacons are fenced in. People cut holes in the fence so they can fish off this side. They can sit right here and no one will see them."

"You'll give them fishing poles," Luz joked.

"It's a perfect spot. They can see who makes it through the mouth of the harbor and who doesn't. Once they're done, they just drop the radio in the water and walk back in."

"What if they shell the harbor?" Luz said. "There's no protection."

Jorge had already thought of that. It was true, but there was nothing to be done. In the silence, the transistor jabbered something about Pacifico beer. He told Felipe to turn it off.

The quiet was a relief.

"It's the only place."

"I suppose," she conceded. "And the station, how do we get inside?"

"The shift changes at seven. We take the new ones before they're settled in."

"All of us?"

"Just myself. There are only two. We don't want a lot of noise."

"How will you kill both of them?" Gloria asked. "Wouldn't it be easier with two?"

"I'm trained to do this."

"And we're amateurs, is that it?"

Yes, he thought, terrible amateurs, but said, "There will be enough to do inside."

"We'll have their guns," Luz said. "That's two extra."

"Which we'll need on the way out."

"So right now," she figured, "in the elevator we have rifles for all five of us."

"Five?" Gloria said.

"Four," Felipe said.

"Three," Jorge said. "The *viejo,* Gloria and myself. Aurelio stays here and takes care of you."

"Five," Luz said. "You saw him this morning—he's better."

"I saw him," Felipe said. "He was still drunk from last night."

"He was ashamed, which means he's found his pride again."

"Then where is he?" Gloria asked.

"Raising cabbages with Teófilo," Felipe joked, and Luz whacked him on the arm.

"*Cabrón!* He's twice the man you are."

"He's proven nothing to me."

"Why are we arguing about this?" Jorge said. "You can't walk."

"I can walk," Luz said, and stood stiffly. She took a few hesitant steps, bent at the waist. "I walk fine."

"Can you run?" Jorge asked. "Can you climb thirteen flights of stairs?"

"I won't have to."

"What if the power's out?"

"I'll stay downstairs with Hector and Francisco. I'll be a visitor. I'll be an old lady waiting for her daughter. That way I can keep an eye on those two."

"We won't wait for you," Gloria said.

"*Qué va,* who asks you to? Give me the shotgun, I'll hold off Clemente's whole army." She hobbled around some to prove her point.

"Sit down," Jorge ordered. "You're making it worse."

She limped to the fireplace, then back at them, the effort plain on her face. "He'll be back. By the virgin, he will."

"Then *he* will take care of you at the station," Jorge said.

"Tonto!" Gloria said, shocked.

"No," Felipe said, "it's stupid."

"Aurelio and no one but Aurelio," Jorge said.

"Fine," Luz said, stopping, and nodded hard to seal the bargain.

"But if he doesn't come back, you stay here."

She didn't answer, and Jorge pressed again.

"Okay," she said. "If he doesn't come back, I stay here."

"Such a melodrama," Felipe said. "Over so little."

"Shut up," Luz said, and finally sat down again. "Now what about upstairs, what happens there?"

IT WAS ALMOST DARK, the wind picking up now, clouds moving in from the sea. Aurelio was still missing, and Jorge asked Felipe to show him to the cave with the radios. Below, everything was quiet; Francisco didn't bother with the password. The day's heat lingered beneath the canopy, dramatic shafts of amber light occasionally breaking through, cutting paths in the gray air, dappling the leaves. Felipe plodded along with his walking stick, the cheaply embossed picture of the tiger on his back wrinkling, winking at Jorge. They crossed a stream and Jorge thought of the officer walled into the creek bank, the pictures of his children. Tomorrow would be long.

They hadn't talked about the retreat, or the tanks, or the possibility that this was just a diversion. He wondered if his grandfather's men had been as determined the night before the Bay of Pigs, though they too must have at least suspected. Had his grandfather felt this helpless? Again Jorge wished the operation were smaller. He wasn't meant to lead, he wasn't born for it, despite his blood. He was almost glad Teófilo had gone AWOL. He didn't want to be responsible for the weak ones—for Hector and Francisco blowing their assignments, for Luz trying to walk on her injured hip. He wondered how far up this helplessness stretched. Did Forbes have a choice, or was it someone else's mission?

It was a weakness of his, wanting everything to be simple. He'd indulged it too much in Miami—the interchangeable waitresses on the beach, on the balcony. The cocaine shared in stairwells, the wrecked Corvette. It was a world that no longer interested him, though at the time it must have seemed real. Or had it? All he could remember was waking up beside Catalina that last morning in El Salvador, then coming ashore here. The year in between didn't exist, or on a level less meaningful than dreams, twitching in your sleep. That's what it was—just reflexes, meat, the jerking of cut nerves. This was different.

A fine sentiment, he thought, but did he really believe this might redeem him? What else did he have? In his note—under the plastic wrap, the envelope taped shut—his father said he was sorry, that he wished it could be different, as if he had no choice in the matter. Now, for the first time, Jorge understood that he had not offered it as an excuse, asking for pity, but calmly, merely acknowledging a truth he'd fought hard but could no longer deny. What a relief, he thought, to give in to what you believe is destiny. It would make everything so much easier. It was not all bullshit, but a large part was, and Jorge pushed it away, concentrated on Felipe's heels sinking into the mud, leaving deep prints.

They came to a fork, and Felipe knelt down and showed Jorge three sticks laid across each other to make an asterisk in the center of one trail. "Aurelio's mark for danger. It's a game we play with the *guardia*. It's the other trail that's mined."

"You think he'll come back?" Jorge asked when they were underway again.

"Aurelio?" He walked on, as if contemplating the question. "I think he's afraid, but I don't think he's a coward. I know he wouldn't leave Luz."

"Can we trust him to take care of her?"

"That's the *only* thing you can trust him to do. It's sad. He was a good *comandante*. If you'd been at the checkpoint, you wouldn't have recognized him. But he's seen too much, he's killed too many. It's a sickness in him."

"You know this sickness?" Jorge asked.

"When I was younger, under your grandfather. In the *federale* I made my peace with those men. I haven't killed since."

"Tomorrow you'll have to."

"That's tomorrow. I can't make my peace with that today. But you, you're trying to, eh?"

"No," Jorge said, "it's the sickness."

"In one so young I didn't think it possible."

"I'm not so young."

"Don't pity yourself. It doesn't inspire me to fight for you—to kill, as you say."

"How should I inspire you?"

"Tell me you have your grandfather's blood. Tell me Cuba should be free. They're both true, no?"

"Yes," Jorge said.

"Then I'm inspired," Felipe said, "but not by your sickness."

Ahead in the dimness rose the bald rock ledge Aurelio had led them over, and Jorge remembered the gully and the curtain of bougainvillea. He was glad the cave wasn't much farther. They'd make it back before it was completely dark. Tonight they'd need their sleep, and he still had to brief everyone, pick the frequencies, double-check the weapons. Rafael and César would want more than just pistols; he might have to persuade them to give up their rifles. Should they eat breakfast or march hungry? He needed to take care of every little detail.

He checked his watch—he had to stop doing that—and just as they topped the rocks, a distant whinny floated up to them from below.

Felipe dropped, went flat, and Jorge had to dive to one side to miss him. He hit the ground wrong, one palm slipping on grit, and banged his chin. It was like getting hit; for an instant he was stunned, breathless. A pebble had bruised his chest, or a button. Felipe patted his shoulder to get his attention.

"Down there," the old man whispered.

The gully was awash in shadows, the sand pocked with prints. In the fading light, it took Jorge a second to pick out the horse. He expected it to be Aurelio's big gelding, but it was a bay mare with a blaze on her forehead. A tall officer rode her slowly up the gully, an AK across his lap, followed by one, two, three others, a fourth horse riderless, nodding along.

"It's him," Felipe said, and Jorge saw the fourth horse was the gelding. He had a body lashed across his saddle, facedown, though from the windbreaker it was clear it was Aurelio. His arms dangled, one sleeve catching in the brush, then falling free. Yoked over the gelding's back were his obsolete radios, bobbing in rhythm.

Jorge's first thought was mercenary: tomorrow they'd have to do everything with the Prick-60. He'd be able to use César in the station. He thought he should be ashamed of his coldness, but he wasn't. It was not his fault it had been drilled into him.

Felipe looked to Jorge as if he could do something, then the two watched the officer turn his bay into the jungle and the others follow after him, disappearing into the black shadows. Jorge lay there waiting until Felipe thought it was safe, thinking of Catalina and the professor and the wages of betrayal. Thinking this was not so different from El Salvador, from Belize, from all the places they'd sent him. He wondered if the *guardia* had caught Aurelio or if he'd turned himself in; if he'd brought them to the cave expecting to be rewarded or they'd tortured him for the location. It made a great difference, though ultimately, he thought, the result was the same.

"*I'LL TELL HER*," FELIPE said on the way back, as if Jorge might argue with him. Jorge thanked him, though he was prepared to do it. While it wasn't his fault, he was responsible; he was willing to bear her sobs, her anger, the knife of her grief—for a short time. Tomorrow he'd be gone. Did he really believe that? No, and yet . . . He was his father's son, he thought, irresponsible, at heart an escape artist.

It was fully dusk out now, stars winking in the canopy. They crept along in the dark, weapons ready, wary of every trail. The jungle trilled with warnings, love calls, screams. Just monkeys. Felipe's tiger flashed white, then vanished again. He told Jorge not to worry. The cavalry didn't like the mountains at night, but it was best to be careful, especially now.

Jorge focused on their soft footfalls, questioning every sound. He thought of Aurelio, those last moments. At least he was clothed. The professor was missing his pants, his wrists wired together behind him. When they lifted the muddy plastic aside, Catalina had patches of hair clawed off, teeth sticking through her lips. He hadn't known the Operator would do this to them, and for the first time he felt the true weight of his betrayal. It was part of the job, he'd thought, though he no longer felt that way. How had he been so cold? And he thought that that other man—that Jorge Ortega—was not him, that for a time he had been insane or taken by a malign spirit, the same as in Miami. How little of his life he could justify.

He'd forgotten about the Operator, the room with the old linoleum he'd only seen empty—three or four layers, their clashing patterns visible in worn spots like strata. He envisioned the squat man squeegeeing the blood toward a corner, a doctor's smock over his beautiful suit, wringing the mop into a bucket filled with what looked like tomato soup.

He bumped into Felipe, who'd stopped, cocking an ear down the mountain.

"Nada," the old man said, and went on.

"Are we close?" Jorge whispered, and Felipe said yes.

They climbed uphill, the trail twisting, passing an asterisk. Water splashed in the distance. Jorge tried not to think but his mind drifted. Maybe it had been quick for Aurelio, the sudden blow of an AK round knocking him out of the saddle. He hoped so. What could they do to you up here, a few horsemen? A beating. At worst, a knife. They were amateurs, not like the Operator, who made appointments, sent apprentices.

"Hear it?" Felipe said.

"The waterfall."

"Let's see if César's sleeping."

It was Francisco, his hat giving him away. César had gone up for supper. "Where are the radios?"

"We had cavalry," Felipe explained.

"How many?"

"Enough."

"Is Rafael back?" Jorge asked.

"No one's come this way."

"Stay awake," Felipe said, and they left him.

The stream in the ravine was lower, and the old man stumbled on the rocks. Jorge caught his arm to steady him, and Felipe yanked it away, swearing.

"It's not you," he apologized.

"What will you tell her?"

"I'll tell her what needs to be told."

"How will the others take it?" Jorge asked.

"Maybe it will shame them into being brave."

"Does it shame you?"

"You?"

"Yes," Jorge said.

"Good," Felipe said, and turned without answering the question.

The blanket was still wet from yesterday; as they ducked into the light of the cave it licked Jorge's arm like a dog's rough tongue. The air smelled of tallow and burnt cooking oil. Luz sat at the table with Gloria and César, eating beans off the tin plates. By the fire leaned Teófilo's AK. Jorge went straight for it.

"Hector found it," Gloria said. She came over and laid a hand on the small of his back as he inspected the weapon. "It was in the rocks. The magazine was full."

"At least he left it for us."

"How thoughtful," she said bitterly. "Where are the radios?"

He looked to Felipe, who'd sat down beside Luz. César had gotten up and was taking his plate outside.

"Let's talk outside," Jorge said, and took her hand.

"Why?"

"Outside."

Luz gave him a concerned look as they left. The blanket flapped back and they were in the dark. Below, César was rinsing his dishes in the pool, and Jorge thought of the officer, his hat toppling over the lip of the dam.

"What happened?" Gloria asked.

Jorge turned her toward the wall, shielding his words from César. He told her about Aurelio.

"Was he with them?"

"We don't know."

"I guess it's best to believe he wasn't."

Jorge agreed.

"He's telling her now?"

"Yes," Jorge said, and tried to remember who had told him about Catalina. He'd forgotten. It hadn't made a great impression on him. It hadn't shocked him, he thought, because he already knew. He hadn't wanted to think about it then, and so he hadn't, though for the next year he thought of nothing else, saw her in every dark-haired woman, followed her down sidewalks, into bars, into beds. In the end he recovered none of her and lost what little was left of himself. Rightfully.

César climbed the stairs in the dark, his dishes dripping.

"How's your arm?" Jorge said, blocking him.

"Fine." He twisted to show Jorge the new bandage.

From inside came a shriek, and then screaming, as if Luz were being attacked.

César dropped his plate and tried to push past, his tin cup still in his hand, but Jorge dug his shoulder in low and lifted him, held him off like a guard. The screaming changed to keening, long drawn-out sobs. César stopped, and so did Jorge, both of them breathing with the effort.

"What is it?" César said.

"Aurelio," Gloria said, and César pulled himself away.

"What happened?"

"We don't know," Jorge said, and told him the whole story.

"The filthy sons of whores."

"Worse," Gloria said.

Inside, Luz had stopped crying. César found his plate. They stood there in the darkness above the pool, listening to the water, the shrilling of the jungle. Jorge looked up to the stars, imagining the weather tomorrow, and Gloria took his hand.

"I'm going down to the waterfall," César said, and Jorge felt bad. "Take these in for me?"

Jorge let go of her hand to take the plate and cup.

When César had disappeared into the ravine, Jorge said, "He's jealous."

"What am I supposed to do?" Gloria said, and kissed him. She tasted of onions and hot sauce, and Jorge was surprised to find he'd become accustomed to her mouth; his tongue knew where the spaces were, slid through them as a fish plies a reef. He pulled her hips against his, the plate against her back.

"You'll do what you want," he said, and she laughed. He dropped the cup and plate and heard them hit and then roll over the edge and splash. In the dark she could have almost been Catalina—her shoulders, her ribs, her nipples. She removed his hands from her chest and kissed his palms.

"Have respect," she said, and she wasn't teasing. "We'll have time."

"Not enough."

"Tonight, I'll make you take me with you."

"I said I would."

"*Mira*, this will make sure."

There was no need, he thought, holding her. He hadn't decided on the basis of one night, or even the two they'd spent together, but on the rest of his life, on the possibility of living with some honor. It was a last gasp, he knew; he would have to quit the business, move to a suburb in the Midwest and live inside, buy a big alarm system and stay away from the windows. It was all so far from here, even Miami, yet he could see it—the trips to the oral surgeon, the nights in the kitchen doing dishes under the track lighting, drinking cheap chardonnay.

Felipe pushed the flap aside, and the light knifed out. He didn't say anything, just gave them a priestly nod—calm and sorrowful—and they followed him in.

Jorge expected Luz to be lying by the fire, but she still sat at the table, bagging shotgun shells, slipping them into a cloth bandolier with fierce concentration.

"I'm going," she told him, the tone almost an insult.

"Hector will help you."

"I don't need any help. I'm going if I have to crawl."

"You're going," Jorge said, to calm her, but when she glanced up from the shells, she gave him a look of utter hatred, as if he had killed Aurelio.

"You're not my *comandante*," she said. "You're nothing but an *americano*, the same as all the others. He warned us about you, and we called him a coward, a traitor. Now look, he was right."

"*Lo siento*," Jorge said. I'm sorry.

"And now I'm going to die for you as well. For believing in you—in America."

Jorge couldn't deny it. No one in Washington cared. The Cold War was over. Castro was dead and there was no need to save face. Money, America's real weapon, would win eventually, and everyone knew it.

"But you'll die," Gloria reasoned with Luz. "You'll go and die with us rather than stay here."

"I'm ready to die."

"And I'm not? He's not?"

"Fine," Luz said. "We'll all die."

"It's bad luck," Felipe warned, "all this talk."

"I don't care," Luz said. "It's the truth, everyone knows it." She finished bagging the shells and got up and hobbled over to the shelf in the wall and brought back the box. It was heavy but no one moved to help her. She sat down and started filling another bandolier, her head bent, muttering to herself. Gloria took the chair beside her and set to work.

"Is César afraid," Luz asked loudly, "to see an old woman cry for her husband?"

"He's checking on Francisco," Jorge said.

"Men are such cowards," Luz informed Gloria, and Gloria—Jorge thanked God—nodded. They counted out the shells like bank tellers.

He and Felipe laid the weapons on his bedroll and doled out the rounds they'd saved. He was glad now for Teófilo's AK; even with Rafael's Mac-10, they were short one rifle. The AKs could take M-16 rounds, which made it easier. There was enough to get in, but they needed real firepower to get out. The ballpark was eight blocks away, and the streets would be full of tanks. Neither of them mentioned El Marichal or the LAW he'd promised, and again Jorge pictured the empty mill, the room blue with cigar smoke, the banker's suit.

"There's seven of us," Felipe noted. "I can do without. Once we're inside, there will be enough."

Jorge tried to argue with him, but he wouldn't be moved. Jorge gave him his pistol, though he only had three clips left. Gloria would get Rafael's Mac-10, Francisco Teófilo's AK. He didn't argue with Luz over the shotgun, a poor choice. She could switch once they were in the building.

They were still doling out rounds when Rafael came in. Everyone turned, as if glad to see him, afraid he too might never return.

"What's all this?" he said, smiling wide, and Luz told him of Aurelio. Rafael went to one knee and took her hand, solemnly nodded and crossed himself, his lips moving. Luz stroked his hair.

"We'll kill them," she said, and tearfully he agreed. "Don't be an old woman. You have lost nothing."

"He was my *comandante*."

"Yes, and now the Ortega is. Tell him what you saw on the road."

He stood and immediately regained his composure, as if his grief was just an act. He was a gypsy, his life built of flourishes. "It's like a parade, the tanks. And rocket launchers, some on trucks."

"How many?" Jorge demanded, and Rafael dug a scrap of paper from his fatigues.

Twenty-two tanks and sixteen rocket launchers, seven of them mounted.

"How many men?"

Rafael turned the paper over. "Thirty-some."

"Thirty men?" Gloria asked.

"Thirty trucks."

"How many in each truck?" Felipe asked.

"It doesn't matter," Luz said. "We'll kill them all."

"They were standing like cattle." Rafael hunched his shoulders to show them.

"Say twenty-five," Jorge said. "That makes a full brigade." And now he was sure the landing was a diversion, that Forbes had decoyed them south out of Mariel. It didn't matter, he supposed; they'd never know.

"All right," he said, and checked his goddamn watch again. "Felipe, go below and tell them to come up. Gloria, go get Hector." He dragged the map over to the table, and Luz had to move her shells. The others didn't budge, as if he had more to say, further instructions. *"Vámonos,"* Jorge ordered. "We've got work to do."

CHAPTER 21

THEY WENT TO BED early, leaving Hector on guard below. At two, César would relieve him. They'd all be up by five. Gloria helped Jorge fold his bedroll and then carried it outside, leading him up above the cave. The jungle had gone quiet, no birds screeching, only the low thrum of insects. Gloria pulled him along.

"Where are we going?" he asked, but she just laughed, let him guess.

She took him through the rocks where they'd watched the train. The valley was spectacular, the lights of Arriaga misting the night sky. The cane was dark. In the black heart of the country, only a tiny pair of headlights glided along, toylike. The still river reflected stars. She laid out the bedroll and pulled her shirt off and he did the same. The wind was chilly but her skin was warm. Her mouth tasted of rum.

"I thought I said no drinking," he said.

She had Aurelio's flask, and he took a burning swig. She laid him down on the rock; it was still warm from the sun. Her lips moved burning over his throat. The wind whipped her hair against his neck, his chest, his belly.

"Wait," he said. "Come here," and she crawled back up and

kissed him, guided his hand down into slickness.

He knew some of her now, enough that returning to her pleased him, filled him with a strange nostalgia. It wasn't Catalina, really. He hadn't been with a woman for more than one night since then, and now he thought it was his fear of sacrilege, of finding someone else, that had prevented him. Gloria was familiar—the scent of her hair, the warmth of her neck, the bowl of her hips. Now, the heat of her surrounding him, he didn't need Catalina. Gloria leaned back, a shadow on a field of stars, her hair tickling his knees. She laughed indulgently, deep in her throat.

"Say you'll take me," she said.

"I'll take you."

"Say I'll be beautiful again."

"You're beautiful now."

"This is nothing," she said. "In Miami I'll break your heart twice a day."

"You're breaking it now."

"Such a liar," she said, then waited for more.

After, the sea breeze cooling their juices, Jorge was ashamed, as if he'd betrayed Catalina. They lay watching the stars. Gloria offered him the rum, but he waved it away.

"Who is this other you think of so much?"

"No one."

"She's prettier than me."

"No."

"You love her better."

"No," he said again.

Gloria laughed. "You lie. Don't look so worried." She took a slug, tipping her head back so her breasts lifted. "Not a wife, I hope."

"No."

"A girlfriend."

"She's dead," Jorge explained.

"*Lo siento.* I speak dishonorably."

"*De nada.* You didn't know."

"No," she said, "one shouldn't speak ill of the dead." She set the flask down on the rock with a clonk and pulled on her shirt. He wanted to tell her to stop, to keep it off, that in a minute he would want her again. She slipped her legs into the bedroll, and he nestled against her. She was stiff, and didn't turn to him. "When you're with me," she said, "you can't think of her."

"I know."

"In Miami, you'll tell me about her. Not now."

He agreed, and she took him in her arms again.

"It's wrong," she said. "I'm not sad for you, only for myself."

Jorge didn't know what to say.

"Don't make me your dead woman. I'll be dead soon enough."

"I don't," Jorge said, but later, when she was sleeping, he knew that neither of them believed that lie.

CHAPTER 22

HE DIDN'T THINK HE'D sleep, yet when he woke, the sky to the east was beginning to lighten, a bold indigo, Venus the morning star low on the horizon, fat as an apple. Clear, a little wind. Forbes was lucky. But it wasn't time yet; the green dial of his watch said four-thirty. Below, night lingered in the valley. The stone was cold, and Jorge wrapped himself around Gloria, her breasts warm inside her shirt. Strands of her hair caught in his whiskers. He kissed her forehead and she flinched and rolled over. He fit his legs behind hers and smelled her neck, pressed against her soft bottom. She grunted, uninterested. It was too early.

He lay there awake, going over streets, details. He played the retreat out like a chess game. In the sub-basement there was a freight elevator that led to a back alley. The ballpark was eight blocks.

Birds were chirping, the sky turning purple. It reminded him of those spring training days, the motel's coachlights still blazing when they left, the wooden bleachers black with dew, the outfield grass tracked with footprints. His father liked to watch the pitchers run. The slow guy's always the ace, he said, as if there were a lesson in it. They kept score, trading the pen every inning; his father's marks were precise, like typing. During the back half of twinighters, Jorge slept against him, his Coke forgotten, going watery at his feet. He woke up in the motel just enough to take his windbreaker off and crawl into the other double. His father had the TV on softly, the sports guy showing highlights of the games they'd just seen.

He wondered if today would even make the national news. Probably just local, a headline in the *Miami Herald,* another failed rebel offensive. But if Forbes was really hitting the north . . . It was pointless thinking about it, and now he wanted to get up, get moving. Gloria stirred and turned to him, muttering something. He bent his head and kissed her wetly on the neck, and she groaned and stretched, an elbow hitting him in the temple.

"Baby," she said, *"lo siento,"* and pulled him against her, eyes still closed, a hand searching for him. "Yes," she murmured, "come on."

The bedroll was thin and the rock hurt his knees and the wind was chilly, but he forgot all that. She opened her eyes and smiled. In her shirt her breasts rose and fell with him. He gritted his teeth.

"Don't close your eyes," she said. "Look at me. Say my name."

He did, but he couldn't stop himself from seeing the shack, that last time, the sun glinting off Catalina's crucifix, spangling the walls, the frozen gecko. Jorge kept his eyes on Gloria's; she dug her nails into his shoulders.

"You're mine," she repeated, rising to meet him. They crashed together, desperate, the slapping not at all comic.

"Gloria," he said.

"Come to me now, my lovely one. Take me to Miami."

"I will," he promised. "I will."

He wanted to be there but he couldn't. That was how it happened, he thought. You forgot what love was, and who you'd been, and then you were alone and nothing was real. Except your father's revolver, once your grandfather's. And you kept that in the Ziploc bag at the top of your closet, under the running shoes you couldn't throw away, and one day, one evening when you could barely think from the night before, you took it apart under the hot desk lamp and then drove around the neon city, slowing your Corvette at stop signs to skip the pieces into the sewer. And then you were alone again and the Marlins were on with the sound down and you had your own pistol out—no one's, a thing without history—sitting in your hand under the lamp like a wish, a promise, and the sweat on the metal smelled like pencil lead and made your fingers slip. And then you forgot that too and now here you are, lost.

He was done and she was crying, biting his shoulder. There was something wrong with him, he thought, and she couldn't save him from it. He felt bad for her, though there was nothing he could do.

"My lovely one," she said. "My darling."

"Yes," he said, "yes," and it was good enough.

It was time now, and they dressed in the wind. She tossed her hair back, tugged her fingers through it, and, oddly, he wanted her. He would keep his promises, he would live his life with honor. It wasn't too late.

Gloria folded the bedroll as he laced his boots. The sun was a bump on the ocean, casting the valley in shadow. Below, the cane fields lay blackened in patches, revealing a neat hatching of canals. Gloria caught him looking at the train tracks but said nothing. He stood and she gave him the bedroll and took his hand and they moved through the rocks and down the mountain, not talking.

CHAPTER 23

DOWN BY THE DAM César was splashing water on his face. He had his shirt off, and his bandage looked clean. He waved up to them, smiling, showing his gold tooth, as if things were finally going their way. In a way it was true, Jorge thought; all he could hear was the trees, the birds calling to each other. Jorge knew the feeling, the lightness, the giddy freedom before the necessity of battening everything down, filtering everything out so there was only one goal. Soon enough, he thought, and waved back, as if wishing him luck. Gloria whistled, and César splashed at them.

The chatter of the radio filled the cave, along with the smell of boiled coffee. The little transistor sat in the middle of the table, between Rafael and Francisco, who were both smoking. Hector was rubbing ointment on his brushburn. Felipe had already gone for the truck. He'd left his windbreaker, which puzzled Jorge. Rafael tipped his head toward the back, where Luz was rummaging through a trunk. She was walking better today but still limping, wincing when she bent over. She gave Jorge a paper bag with a pair of chinos and a billowy silk shirt; he turned away to change into them—the pants loose and too long, a grease stain on the shirt's collar—then worried the pockets wouldn't fit his K-bar, let alone his field glasses, the plastique.

"You carry this bag," Luz explained, and Gloria laughed at him. It was a bad sign; he really hadn't thought of it. Hell, he thought, it was early.

"What about my boots?"

"You'll need them," Luz said, as if no one would notice.

There was no clever way to disguise the weapons; the sawed-off was fine, but the rifles were a problem, especially the M-16s. They'd have to wrap them in blankets, pretend they were mike stands or lamps or something. It was only two blocks, he thought, and half of that was the park. Still, it was a risk, with the city on alert. He'd leave his with Gloria and go in with just his pistol and the knife. When he was done, they'd hustle them across the street. Once they were inside it didn't matter.

"How will we hide the guns?" he asked Luz.

"*Qué va*, it's not all perfect. We'll need some luck. It's a little thing."

"A bullet is a little thing," Gloria said, wrapping a shawl over her shoulders.

"I can't take care of everything," Luz said.

"Mine's not a problem," Rafael said, and showed Gloria how to hide the compact Mac-10 under her shawl. He folded the stock on Teófilo's AK so Francisco could slip it under Felipe's big windbreaker.

"There are still these two," Jorge said, pointing to the sixteens.

Rafael looked at them with his hands on his hips, then just shrugged. "What do you expect, American guns."

"We need them."

Luz hefted one, tipped it down and measured it against her leg; it was too long.

Gloria took it from her. "We don't need them till we're inside."

They all nodded.

"Why can't someone bring them across the street in a box?"

"Where are you getting this box?" Francisco asked.

"From the *mercado*, or from the truck. Surely they have boxes large enough."

"For fish," Hector said. "They pack them with ice to ship to Arriaga. One should fit both of them."

"There you are," Rafael said, as if he'd thought of it, and patted Jorge on the back and sat down again.

César came in, his hair dripping. On the radio, an old soca tune faded and the morning guy punched in a promo for Bustus Domecq—a skit with rude sound effects—and Francisco laughed. "I'd like to meet that guy."

"Sure," Luz said. "We'll just wait till tonight. *Stupido.*"

Rafael shushed them. He turned to Jorge. "How long?"

The second hand seemed to be flying. "Five minutes."

Luz took César and Hector back by the fire to get them some clothes. Francisco double-checked his ammunition, the clips bulging like rocks in the windbreaker's pockets. Gloria practiced walking naturally with the Mac-10. Rafael just sat at the table, smoking and sipping his coffee, and Jorge was glad he'd made the right choice. He dragged his pack over to a chair and thumbed in the locks' combinations.

"How will I speak to you?" Jorge quizzed him, digging through his gear.

"On the walkie-talkie." He picked it up and recited what they'd decided last night. "I speak to you through the big radio. Every helicopter I see, every landing craft that makes it into the harbor, I tell you. And where Clemente's tanks are positioned, and his men. Calmly, in a clear voice. I repeat everything. 'Repeat,' I'll say, and tell you again."

"How will you know I understand?"

"You say 'Copy.'" He was bored.

"And when I don't understand."

"You say "'Come again.' But here, I have a question."

"What?" Jorge said, and looked up from the neatly wrapped plastique.

Rafael held the transistor and pointed to the little ribbed door in the back. "You have extra batteries, yes?"

"Nine-volt. The dumb square ones."

"No," Jorge said. He took the radio from him and switched it off.

"Hey," Rafael said, laughing, "we'll get some tomorrow, eh?"

Jorge laid the plastique in the bag, his field glasses and his Marine survival knife on top of it, then covered them with a dirty T-shirt. They fixed Rafael's pack, folding the Prick-60's sectioned antenna so he could set it up quickly. Felipe's nephew would have breadfruit for him, and a fishing pole, and a bucket for his catch. The harbor would be crawling, Jorge thought. Clemente would be ready.

"Okay," Jorge said so everyone could hear, and they stopped and looked to him as if he'd make a speech.

He recognized the silence; in El Salvador that morning Catalina had waited for him to say something, the professor stood rigidly at attention, as if to prove he wasn't afraid. And in the end he wasn't. They'd had to burn the answers out of him, the bastards, cranking the field telephone so it jangled, the wires crackling on his charred thighs. Catalina hadn't been any easier.

Now he couldn't find anything inspiring to say. For Santa Rosa? For my grandfather? For my father? My mother? It had been years since he'd believed in anything, least of all himself. America. Cuba. Freedom. The people. Words were nothing, and wishes. The same with regret. There was only the day ahead, the work to be done.

He went through his troops one by one, almost a roll call, asking if they were ready, if they knew what to do. *"Esta listo?"* It went quickly, the answers quiet, identical, emotionless.

"César," he said, "you lead. Rafael second, then Hector and Gloria. Luz, you're with me and Francisco."

César helped Rafael with his pack and pushed the blanket aside with the barrel of his M-16, the sun spilling in. They left the fire going, cards splayed out on the table, chairs knocked back, coffee still steaming. They left Jorge's pack and his bedroll and his clothes. He let the flap fall and took Luz under one shoulder, Francisco shoring up the other.

The stairs were tricky, uneven. Gloria looked back to make sure they were okay. Her face had gone grim, eyes wired, lips pinched like a killer's. Birds were screaming in the canopy. The light lay in patches and scraps on the pool, winking with the breeze. As they made their way down, Jorge caught a glimpse of César's plate glinting on the bottom, shining up at him like a hubcap. Ahead, César and Rafael were just figures in the ravine, ragged silhouettes in a tunnel, the sun at the end a blinding white. It would be a hot day, he thought. A long, hot day.

CHAPTER 24

"WAIT," JORGE SAID, and Gloria stopped and looked back at him. The sweat shone on her neck. She called down to Hector, who told Rafael, who stopped César.

"I'm all right," Luz said, and held up one hand as if to prove it, but she was gasping, her eyes bright with pain. Francisco looked to Jorge for a decision. They were below the main trail now, on an old logging road, no more than a long rut of orange mud. Far down the valley, the sun perched on the city skyline—the station, the office buildings, the ruined hotels. In the fields, lone banyan trees threw reaching shadows. It was all taking too long, and Luz knew it.

"*Vámonos,*" she said. "Go. Felipe's waiting for you."

"It's not far," Jorge lied.

"I can't go any further." She sat down in the mud and bowed her head.

"You said you'd crawl."

"I was wrong."

He bent down and took her under the arm. "Pick her up," he told Francisco, and the two of them lifted her.

"Idiots!" she said. "Leave me."

Jorge ignored her. "Here," he said, and showed Francisco how to make a chair of their arms.

"It's stupid," Luz said.

"Go," he told Gloria, over her protests.

Luz was light but the mud sucked at their ankles. Francisco staggered, his cigarette breath wafting foul across her lap. She was still muttering and swearing at them, as if it were all their fault. Jorge wanted to check his watch, to see how far behind they were. They needed to be on the air by 0720. He'd built in a cushion, but that was already gone.

As they trudged down the ruts, the bag flapped against his hip, and he wished he'd brought his pack. Ahead, Gloria took a step and sank in up to her calf. She looked back at Jorge, only half amused, and for a minute she was Catalina turning on her burro under the power lines, the dust from the professor's mount shrouding her face.

How gauzy memory was, how solid. He visited that day like his own private island, hiding from the rest of the world, as if replaying their conversations could make them alive again. It had tortured him so long it was almost a comfort.

"Which one?" the professor said, and Jorge always picked the same tower. The bolts bled rust onto the concrete base; it was pitted, and a water bug skated across a meager puddle. Catalina got off and helped him unpack the plastique. It was gray and rubbery, chemical-smelling, a kind of deadly Play-Doh. There was enough for three of the four feet. They each fashioned a softball-sized glob around the lowest bolt. Jorge had them stand clear as he thumbed in the blasting caps. He paid out the det cord, walking backward up the hill, then went down again and connected it. The professor kept watch with his carbine, expecting the army to sweep down on them at any second. Jorge had to fake his nervousness; the area militia had strict orders to stay away, to give them enough time to escape. He walked back up to Catalina, who was holding the wires far apart.

"They can touch," he said. "Nothing will happen."

In his pack he had a set of clackers for a claymore. He wired them and gave one to her, one to the professor.

"What do we do?" the professor said, and Jorge said, "Blow it up."

It had been a year now—more—yet he could see the red flush his beard left on her neck, feel the post of her earring click against his teeth. He could hear himself saying her name in the tin shack that morning, that last time, and then he remembered leaving police headquarters a few days later, walking out into the cinder-block hall where a clutch of guards were swigging Orangina and smoking cheap cigarettes, reading the *futbol* scores to each other. They shut up, went to attention and parted for him because he was the American, and famous today, the rebel leaders safely in custody. He wanted one of them to say something funny so he could punch him and not stop until they beat him to his knees.

That was all long gone, he thought, pulling his foot free of the mud. Gone like his father and the autographed balls he kept on his dresser, signed by dead men. Like his mother, her birthday checks mailed from Iowa, each one larger than the last, as if she were giving him a raise merely for surviving another year without her. Gone, all of it. There was today, the next few hours, the next step. It was what he liked about the job, the immediacy, the necessity of concentrating on small things. He'd been better at it once, more dedicated, less scatterbrained. It was funny—even that was gone.

They were into the foothills. The road gave way to a packed dirt trail, almost level. Luz was getting heavy; Francisco's eyes pleaded with him. Jorge stopped the column, and César and Rafael came back to take their places, Hector moving forward to point. He checked his watch: they were five minutes behind. They'd make it up in the truck. According to Felipe's directions, it was only another three hundred meters.

The canopy thinned, the sun hot on Gloria's hair, making him squint. They skirted a field of head-high corn, the tough leaves reaching out to score their arms. The ground was soft underneath their feet, and the air smelled of manure. They were supposed to turn at the end of the row and follow an irrigation ditch. Jorge halted them, a hand in the air, and poked his head around the corner. Ahead, as promised, stood a rusted quonset hut.

"I'll check it," he told them, and left his bag with Gloria. He ducked into the corn with his sixteen, keeping low, the leaves batting at his face. When he drew even with the hut he saw the truck tucked inside, and Felipe beside it with a much younger man in overalls and a Yankees cap, both of them smoking cigarillos.

"*Cabrón*," Jorge called, and stepped from the corn, his rifle at his side so as not to alarm the nephew. The quonset smelled of motor oil and old hay.

"You get lost?" Felipe said.

Jorge shouted for the others to come, then explained.

The nephew's name was Moises. The bill of his Yankees cap was ragged, the white *N Y* dirty. He shook Jorge's hand like a Marine.

"Look," Felipe said. He reached into the cab and pulled out an AK with a homemade wooden stock.

Jorge said he could keep the pistol, but Felipe insisted on giving it back, along with the clips.

"You can't fight with it," he said, to cap his argument, then turned his attention to Luz, who arrived between César and Rafael like a queen.

"I'm fine," she insisted, but it took three of them to get her into the bed of the truck.

The nephew had taken care of everything. He had beautiful breadfruit for Rafael's pack, a bamboo pole and a wicker creel, and a canteen for them to share. The truck was an old GMC, the grill lumpy as a bulldog's face. All eight of them fit comfortably under the platform of empty melon boxes. He'd wired full crates on top and thrown a musty tarp over the whole thing, cinching it tight with clothesline. Inside it was dark except for a sliding window which looked into the cab, giving them a view over the hood of the brilliant cornfields. When Moises got in, he opened the window and asked if everyone was all right.

"*Bueno*," Jorge said.

"At the checkpoint," Moises said, "just put that box over the window."

It wasn't a whole box, just one side, a waxed slab of cardboard with a smiling melon on it. *Product of the People's Republic of Cuba*, it said. The melon was wearing a cap like Castro's.

Moises eased the truck out of the quonset, and Jorge had to grab on to the window frame. Luz grunted, and Gloria held her steady. They bumped over a pipe and swung onto a dusty road, rocks thunking in the undercarriage. The floor was hard and smelled of rotten pulp, and the mud from their boots stank. Jorge leaned closer to the window to breathe the fresh air. Cornfields ran on both sides, split by ditches.

"You're from Miami," Moises said over the engine, as if Jorge might know friends of his. "I've always wondered what it's like."

Jorge thought of how as a child he'd wanted more than anything to see Santa Rosa—the beaches, the ballpark, the formal gardens. They were stunning, yes, but the first time he'd come he was struck by the slums, the jobless wandering the hot streets, the open sewers, the pollution. Or was it just him, heir to the family penchant for disaster? He'd lived with the dead too long, loved them too much.

"It's beautiful," Jorge said. "You wouldn't believe the money there."

"I've seen the cars on television." He slowed for a paved road ahead—old blacktop gone gray, the cracks filled with meandering lines of sealer. The tires climbed the lip; he was trying to be gentle with them. As the truck lurched and then settled heavily, a shot went off, deafening under the tarp.

"Weapons on safety!" Jorge yelled, but in English, as if he were back at the Langley range. He switched over, screaming even louder. "Anyone hit?"

In the silence, he could hear Moises searching for third, the linkage clinking.

"It was mine," Hector said, apologizing. "It went straight up."

"*Culo,*" Felipe said.

"Is it on safety now?" Jorge scolded.

"Yes."

"Keep it on till we're in the building. That goes for everyone." He looked through the window, still pissed off. The blacktop ran straight through the fields.

"Goddamn," he said.

"Everyone okay?" Moises asked.

Jorge didn't see how Forbes expected him to do this, realistically. It had to be a diversion. Forbes had counted on him *wanting* to do it. Santa Rosa, his grandfather. The psychology was cheap; he knew Jorge couldn't resist it.

He lifted his watch to the light.

"A little faster," he asked Moises, and the truck surged.

"You know the car Don Johnson drives—the Barracuda?" Moises asked. "Now that is a beautiful car."

He drove as if to show he deserved it, a connoisseur of the road. The tarp fluttered and snapped in the wind. There was no traffic, or only the occasional Volkswagen coming the other way, an old man on a bicycle, a dying tractor coughing across. Corn and cane, miles of it. The signs that flashed past were homemade. Moises cut the curves, drifting into the other lane to keep his speed up. They were on time now, even a little in the black. Bony cows gazed forlornly at them, scratched their necks on fenceposts. Moises sang an old Wailers tune: *Baby don't worry, 'bout a thing, 'cause every little thing, gonna be all right.* In back they were silent, blinking in the dark. Hector kept apologizing, until Luz told him to shut up.

At a crossroads, they slowed. On the corner a skinny black man in a flowered apron was cooking strips of meat on a brazier, waving a serving fork to flag down customers. Moises eased the truck up onto a wide highway—the Arriaga road. It was newer, a white stripe down the center, wooden guardrails crossing little bridges. Another car Jorge couldn't place sped along ahead of them. Moises ran the truck right up to its bumper, then braked. Ahead was an even slower car; they were part of a train. A filling station came, and a busy cantina.

"You can put the box up now," Moises warned Jorge, and he did.

Moises knocked three times, and Jorge pulled the box aside, the light blinding.

"I'll do that so you know it's okay."

Jorge replaced the box and leaned his back against it. In the dark, someone flicked a switch.

"Weapons on safety," Jorge ordered.

"But what if—" César started.

"Shut up," Luz said. "Do as he says."

They slowed suddenly, Francisco pitching on top of him, the box slipping, letting in a slice of light. They stopped and Jorge fixed it. Jorge could hear voices, boots scratching on grit. A car passed the other way, shifting up. After a long minute, Moises crunched into first and moved forward.

Jorge waited for someone to cough, sneeze, giggle, but there was nothing, not even breathing. The truck idled, thrumming. Outside, a car door clicked open, a trunk thunked shut. A man asked if there was any contraband; another man answered with a laugh, as if it were an impossibility.

Jorge leaned against the cardboard and imagined the eight of them hauled out and shot by the roadside, piled facedown in a ditch, the picture grainy in the morning paper, their rifles laid out like an arsenal. He imagined them hustled into á truck at bayonet point, their wrists tie-wrapped behind them. Waiting in a damp cell for the interrogator. Days of mealy rice and blindfolds, knees driven into kidneys, rods on the soles of their feet.

Moises pulled up and stopped, then killed the engine. His door opened and the truck lifted a bit as he jumped out. It dipped again as someone climbed into the cab and popped the dash, riffling papers. Like a child, Jorge closed his eyes, as if that would make him invisible.

"Yankee fan?" a man asked, and Moises mumbled something.

"Where are you going?" another, sterner voice asked.

In the cab, a hand knocked against the window right beside Jorge's ear, rapped as if testing it. A shiver like rain crossing water shot through his skin, exiting his fingertips.

The window slid open. A hand pressed against the box, and Jorge tried not to actively push back.

He imagined grabbing the man by the throat and snapping his windpipe with his thumbs like they'd shown him in Quantico. It wouldn't help them; Moises was outside. Who knew how many there were? Now he wished Moises hadn't cinched them in.

"Okay," the stern man called.

The pressure lessened. The hand retreated, the window closed.

The truck lifted as the man got down.

It sank again, and the door clunked shut. The engine caught, and Moises put it in first and they started off. He kicked it up to second, then third. Still no one said anything. Jorge kept the box against the window, waiting for Moises to knock.

Fourth, neatly. *Baby don't worry,* Moises sang, *'bout a thing.*

Jorge knocked three times, and Moises answered. He lowered the box and Moises slid the window open.

"Lo siento," Moises said. "I forgot."

"Don't do that," Jorge said, and Moises laughed.

Ahead, the road was empty, Santa Rosa towering in the distance. Jorge checked his watch: they were right on time, but he didn't tell anyone this. *"Arriba,"* he said, and Moises pointed the truck for the city and put his foot down, and they rocketed along, headed directly into the rising sun.

CHAPTER 25

THE FIRST BAD SIGN was the tank under the viaduct. It was Russian and painted for the jungle. They were still a mile outside the city. Jorge almost didn't see it; Moises pointed it out. All he could see was a few feet of barrel, a tread tucked under a scarred archway. They drove through its field of fire, maintaining speed.

It wasn't a show of force, just a textbook defense. The tank would tie up the road, slow the assault, keep them from reaching Arriaga too easily. It surprised Jorge that Clemente was ready for a successful landing. He'd have the ballpark covered, the soccer stadium, the beaches—anyplace they could land a number of choppers.

Jorge thought of the retreat and swore.

"What is it?" Gloria asked.

"A tank."

"Are we that close?" Luz asked, and he wondered if she knew the strategy.

An old Citroën whipped by them, a Lada tailing it. Another highway ran alongside theirs; it was busy, trucks barreling nose to tail, one hauling a pyramid of chickens in filthy wooden cages.

Jorge laughed and Hector asked what it was.

"A good sign," Jorge told them.

He'd thought Clemente would close the roads. He expected the downtown streets empty, storefronts shuttered and boarded up with plywood, the only pedestrians squads of *guardia,* but the sidewalks were hopping, people making their way to work, packs jostling at the corners. At first Jorge thought it was just good luck, then recognized it as a deliberate tactic; Clemente would make them kill civilians. Again, it was a textbook defense—make the population a barrier. The professor would be indignant.

It was Monday, garbage trucks double-parked, hazards blinking. The stoplights were still all cautions. Moises was tentative, a country boy. A few blocks ahead, a Saracen slipped across an intersection behind a bus and disappeared. Jorge wished he could see the roofs. They passed a tank in the entrance of a parking garage, the driver's head poking out of a hole forward of the turret; he was drinking coffee with a headset on, *La Figueroa* spread before him on the deck. Secretaries and clerks filed past him, oblivious, and Jorge thought that Aurelio had been right—the war had been going on too long.

They turned into the side streets, the buildings giving way to stucco bungalows and brick apartment buildings, seagulls perched on cornices. The sun cut through alleys, lay in bright stripes across the pavement. There seemed to be a stop sign at every corner. Moises assured him it was the quickest route.

A right, a left, and the sky opened up before them, the sea invisible beneath it. The *mercado* was teeming, the booths' white awnings flapping in the breeze. Someone had a radio going, a pair of marimbas plinking away. Moises had to wait for a stake truck crowded with pigs, then cut another off, prompting a honk. He swung the GMC jolting over a curb and bumped down an alley strewn with the gray bones of crates and smashed, weathered vegetables. Graffiti swerved along the brick walls—*The People Now, Martí!; Che Is Dead*—all the taunts and promises of the revolution. Moises braked, throwing Jorge against the window, and tugged the truck left, angling for a windowless garage door, the back entrance of some factory, its banks of windows opaque as if blanched from years of steam.

They stopped and Moises hopped out and threw the door up with a clatter, then came back and pulled the truck into the blackness and rolled the door closed again.

"Well, we made it," Luz joked, as if it had been in doubt.

Jorge wanted to ask about her hip, but didn't. She was with them, that was enough. Moises fought with the clothesline, throwing it over the top. When he finally lifted the tarp they had to shield their eyes.

The building was an old fire station, the walls festooned with horse tack and dusty hoses, the brass fittings ripped off for salvage. The truck fit neatly between riveted girders.

It took four of them to help Luz down.

"It's too far," she said, but Jorge ignored her and she cracked the sawed-off Ithaca and thumbed in a pair of shells.

First thing, Jorge sent Moises out to find a crate for the sixteens.

Rafael shouldered his pack, and Hector arranged the breadfruit on top of the Prick-60. With his silly muttonchops, he looked the part of a vendor, practically typecast.

"You know how to shout?" Francisco asked.

"Oye, oye!" Rafael tried. "Sweet as water!"

Francisco showed him how to hold the fruit up, three in each hand. "Can you juggle?" he asked, but Rafael couldn't. Gloria gave him the bamboo pole and arranged the creel against his hip.

Jorge consulted his watch and hustled Rafael to the door, double-checking everything. He gave Rafael his field glasses and ran through the frequencies. Rafael clicked the transistor and got a mambo tune.

"Can I have some cigarettes?" he asked, and Jorge realized he'd forgotten them back with his pack.

"Ah well," Rafael said. He patted Jorge on the arm. "Good luck, Ortega."

Luz hobbled over and gave him a kiss, then Gloria.

Rafael turned to the rest and gave them a wave, then Jorge lifted the door and Rafael ducked under and Jorge closed it again, only to hear a knock on it.

It was Moises with a crate, the naked wood stained dark in spots with fish blood. The sixteens fit, but the crate was heavy. With his arm, César couldn't carry it. Felipe brushed Hector aside and lifted it easily.

The park was two blocks.

"Hector, you go first," Jorge instructed. "Luz, you and César next." He put Francisco with Felipe; Gloria would stay with him. None of them objected, though he was ready to defend his choices. From now on, his every decision meant life or death. As soldiers they accepted that; he'd seen it in El Salvador and Honduras, in Nicaragua and Belize—all over the globe, he suspected—yet it always astonished him. He had too many questions to simply accept anything, especially the idea that he of all people was leading them. He imagined his grandfather offshore that last morning, the landing craft speeding for the Bay of Pigs. What had he said to his men? Did he have to say anything? They all knew what the job was. The less said the better. It didn't make it a mystery, just something shared between them, understood at a level deeper than words.

"Okay," Jorge said, and motioned toward the door.

Moises gave his uncle a hug, Luz held Gloria to her. As Luz embraced him, Jorge watched César kneel and kiss Gloria's hand; she laid her other one to his cheek.

"Okay," Jorge said again, "in the park everyone waits for me—no matter what."

He looked around to make sure they understood, then lifted the door and let Hector out. Jorge gave him a minute. They waited in line silently, ducking under in pairs. Jorge patted Felipe's back as he passed, the crate balanced on one shoulder.

Jorge closed the door, and Gloria took his hand. It was their turn. He had his bag with everything in it. Her thumb rubbed the sweat on his palm and she gave him a surprised look. He bent and lifted the door and they ducked into the light. He turned to close it, but Moises stopped him and flung it up again, the rollers clattering in the track.

They both looked back, puzzled.

"Forgive me," he said, as if they'd understand. "I really can't stay."

LUZ WAS TOO SLOW. They bunched up behind her, lingering at stalls, fingering marrows and tubers, white carrots. A few *guardia* were out, strolling the *mercado* in pairs, but Clemente was keeping the reinforcements out of sight. The sky was quiet, not a single chopper flitting between the high-rises. Jorge sauntered toward the end of the row, shopping, Gloria holding on to his arm like a wife. They passed a stall with buckets of squid, urchins in purple ink. The man at the scale had a boom box tuned to the morning guy's annoying voice.

Ahead, Felipe and Francisco turned the corner, the crate on the old man's shoulder like a child's coffin. Jorge hesitated a second, then followed, crossing the cobblestones, Gloria keeping up with him. Jorge remembered the street from before. The mannequins were gone, and the smashed glass; the store windows were boarded up, already graffiti'd with the initials of splinter groups. Far down the block, palms nodded over the stone entrance of the park. There were no *guardia* at all. Felipe and Francisco had already made it in.

He tried not to run, but when they turned through the archway and onto the curving path, he hurried past the stone benches, his bag brushing the hibiscus, petals snowing down. An older couple came the

134

other way, the woman carrying a tiny dog in the crook of one arm. Gloria squeezed his hand, and Jorge slowed. They were supposed to be lovers, and though they were, he was afraid they were unconvincing, the knife clearly visible inside his bag, the pistol, the clips.

"*Buenas dias*," the old man said, bowing.

"*Buenas tardes*," Jorge said, and walked on.

They were waiting in the same corner Felipe had shown him, all of them crouching down behind the wall. Across the street, beneath the marquee, one of the doors was open, a guard leaning out, smoking a cigarette. The morning guy jabbered from the speakers, passersby turning to find the voice. The booth Bustus Domecq had broadcast from was empty—a relief. Jorge lifted the dirty T-shirt and found the knife and set it on top. He checked his watch, then clicked the safety off his pistol. He was surprised Clemente was letting them get this close, that he hadn't at least scrambled his MiGs and Werewolves. The idea that this was all just a diversion took him again, but there was no time to think about it, which was good.

"You know the signal," he asked Gloria, and she told him what it was. She kissed him, not hard, in fact with almost no passion, as if it might interfere. As he scuttled along the wall with his bag, Felipe slapped him on the arm for luck, and Jorge thought the whole mission was a mistake, that they would all be killed for nothing.

He straightened up at the path, carrying the bag in his left hand so he could dip into it with his right and find the knife. The front entrance of the park was another arch; people were passing, hurrying to work with handbags and purses and briefcases. Traffic was light, which he appreciated; he didn't want to run across. When he reached the arch, he stopped, waiting for the guard to flick his cigarette into the street. He needed them both inside, behind the tinted glass. The guard scanned the street and dragged on the butt, smoking it like a roach. He was small and dark, clean-shaven. Jorge moved to the curb, trying not to watch him. The building reared above him, the identical rows of windows; he didn't bother counting the stories. He wondered how Rafael was doing. That was where all the hardware would be, down by the harbor.

The guard plucked the butt from his mouth and tossed it like a dart onto the sidewalk, where a woman in red purposely skirted it.

Jorge waited for a blue Yugo and started across, the bag swinging from one fist.

He joined the flow of pedestrians on the other side, casually passing the wall of tinted windows. He cut behind a fat man in an apron and a Pirates cap, sliding closer to the building, then slipped into the marquee's shadow. He chose the door the guard had been leaning out of, hoping it would still be open.

It was.

The guard who'd been smoking was bent over a water cooler, the other sitting behind a waist-high desk, sipping coffee. A stretch of white marble floor separated the two. It was a gift, and Jorge didn't hesitate. Even as he strode toward the closest one, he was calculating where he would move after he stabbed him. He used the man's body to shield himself from the other one, to hide what he was doing. His hand squeezed the rubberized grip; with one step left, he yanked the knife back.

The man looked up from the bubbler, surprised to see him. He opened his mouth to speak, and Jorge swung the knife underhanded—hard, in an arc, like pitching a softball—and planted it in his stomach, ripping upward, then let go as the man fell forward onto it.

He grabbed the pistol and let the bag drop, turned and caught the flash of the other's uniform and fired—and kept firing, steadily, running straight at the desk, counting the rounds. There was an open el to his left; he could sense the space there, the elevators maybe, but he needed to keep his eyes on the guard.

The man was sprawled on the floor, hit, though Jorge couldn't tell where, the blood shiny on the marble. He was a big man with a mustache—alive, his eyes open. Jorge pumped two quick ones into his gut, then dropped to one knee and spun to his left. A woman was sitting at a desk in front of the elevators, her hands raised before her face, shaking, as if to keep him away.

She was a receptionist, a nametag above one breast. Her mouth was moving but she wasn't saying anything. A startle effect, shock; Jorge had seen it before. He walked up to her, aiming at her face. Though she hadn't touched the phone, his first impulse was to blow her away, keep things simple. She was young, with long dark hair and a cross on a chain, and Jorge noticed the pistol was shaking.

"On the floor!" he ordered. He had to do it again, pushing her down, then ripped the phone from the jack.

A number flashed above one elevator, freezing him. It was on 9, coming down. He waited, listening to the rush of traffic outside. It stopped on 6, then stayed there.

"Don't move!" he warned her, and ran around the el to the front doors. His bag lay on the floor beside the first guard, the puddle already claiming it. He hid the pistol behind his back, cracked the door a few inches, and stuck his head out.

It was bright, and he realized the building was air-conditioned. Above, from the speakers in the marquee, the morning guy droned on, some plug for a brand of flour. People passing stared at Jorge like he might be someone famous from the radio. Maybe so, he thought. He smiled and waved, like he was saying hi to the entire world.

CHAPTER 27

AGAIN, IT WAS HIS decision—who would accompany him upstairs and who would most likely die. He only needed two people. He chose Gloria and Felipe, as he knew he would. Love and honor. Luz didn't seem bothered by it. She sat behind the bloody desk, the shotgun across her lap. The guards had AKs, so everyone had the rifle they liked. They'd barred all the doors and set up security by the elevators. The receptionist was in the women's bathroom, in a locked stall, bound with silver duct tape. Outside, traffic ground by. According to the clock on the wall, the landing would start in five minutes. In fifty they could leave, though none of them believed it.

There was no time for goodbyes. Jorge summoned the elevator, and they waited, weapons drawn in case it held someone.

It didn't, and they got on and Jorge pressed the button for 13. The doors closed and the cable sang above them, the numbers turned. They still had a few civilians to get through—the engineer and the DJ at the very least—but they could finesse them, just intimidate them with the guns. He made a show of clicking the safety on his sixteen. Felipe and Gloria both had AKs; they were used to the Russians.

"No shooting," he reminded them. "I want everything quiet."

The light disappeared behind the brushed-steel panel, then resurfaced under the 9. He was surprised at how easily he'd killed the two men, and puzzled why he hadn't lit up the receptionist. He would have when he was younger.

The last dead person he'd seen was the professor. It had shamed him, his living after that. This was a different feeling; he couldn't say exactly how right now. It wasn't that it was justified. There was no time for that now—for Catalina, really. He needed to be clear, to shed that past, at least for the next fifty minutes. After that, he promised, he would serve her again. And his father, yes, with his shrine of the TV, his gospel of the sprayed wallpaper. Why did they doubt him now, Jorge thought. Hadn't he been faithful so far?

Above, the 12 pinged and they slowed, his stomach flipping. Gloria and Felipe hugged the sides of the doors, primed to spin through. Jorge knelt against the back wall, ready to take anyone head-on. They eased into 13.

The doors rolled open on an empty hall. He'd expected another receptionist at a desk, but there was just wood paneling, the directions to the studio and the manager's office on a fat gold plaque. A reggae tune was chunking from the low ceiling. They got off, their rifles at their sides. Jorge followed the arrow pointing to the studio. He kept to one wall, Gloria trailing him against the other, Felipe walking drag opposite.

Intelligence had done a good job. All the offices were locked; people didn't come in till nine. The hall turned, the reggae dragging on through another chorus. The air-conditioning was freezing. They passed a few empty studios, dark behind venetian blinds, microphones craning over tables. It was a big station for a city this size, overpowered, operating around a hundred thousand watts. You could pick it up in Miami, though Jorge never did.

Ahead, stripes of light fell across the carpet, and Jorge stopped Gloria with a hand and crouched down. The song was fading, repeating the same line. Jorge wanted to take the DJ when he was off the air, then pretend it was a special report on the invasion, an update from Havana, the facts sketchy, incomplete. He had a minute left when they went to a commercial for shaving cream.

He crawled beneath the window to the edge of the door, the carpet burning his elbows. Gloria followed, then Felipe. The commercial segued into station identification, and Jorge heard the muffled crunch of explosions in the distance.

They bloomed like thunder, flowered, rolled, shook. He was pleased and for once thought more of Forbes. Maybe they'd really do it. Free Cuba. It was a fantasy, yet here they were.

He concentrated on the jingle, waiting for the DJ to introduce the next song. There was no segue—a guitar started, a steady backbeat behind it, and Jorge nodded to Gloria. She reached up for the doorknob, got a grip on it and checked his eyes again. Felipe was ready. Jorge held up three fingers. They nodded.

One. Two.

Gloria threw the door open and Jorge broke in, racing around a table and jabbing his sixteen at a man with a headset. The man fell back out of his chair, the cord spilling his coffee, the mug bouncing on the carpet. Jorge stuck the barrel in his face and the man turned his head, gave him his neck like a whipped dog.

Felipe had the engineer standing, hands up, behind a complicated mixing board. Gloria pushed the AK into his chest.

"On the floor," she ordered, and the engineer went to his knees.

"Take the headset off," Jorge told the DJ, and heard his own words echoed in the hall a second later.

Just then—too late—he recognized the rock song. It wasn't a song at all, just a jingle for Pacifico beer. It had stopped. They were live on the air.

He hit the cough button and swore.

With his free hand, he grabbed the DJ by the shirt and yanked him up and shoved him against the table. A stack of labeled cassettes clattered across the top. "Play something," Jorge hissed, and the man fumbled with a cassette and jammed it into a player. The leader ran. Jorge let go of the cough button and closed the mike.

It was the same reggae song.

The DJ backed toward the corner. Jorge hit him with the butt of the sixteen in the gut and he crumpled to the floor. Jorge squeezed the rifle's pistol grip, fighting the urge to kill him, to kick his face in. The man was weeping, curled on the carpet, knees drawn up, giving him his spine, and Jorge thought how easily he could paralyze him with one kick. It was insane, and he turned away, dazed, as if he'd been hit. Across the room, Gloria and Felipe were taping the engineer's ankles together.

"This one too," Jorge said, and laid his sixteen on the table. In the hall the reggae tune went on incessantly. Far off, the barrage thudded. Jorge smoothed his hair back with both hands, trying to calm down. First things first, just as they said in basic. He had to get Rafael.

As intelligence promised, there was a general coverage receiver, which picked up everything from FM to shortwave. It was a new ICOM, top of the line, and Jorge dialed in the frequency they'd agreed on, grabbed a patch cord and ran a pair of headphones over to the table.

Nothing but static, a noisy wash of electrons.

He put on the DJ's pair and twisted one earpiece so he could listen to both of them. The reggae tune was into its third chorus, out of sync with the hall speaker. Gloria and Felipe were dragging the engineer outside, and he motioned for them to shut the door.

Jorge shuffled through the cassettes, unsure which the DJ had already played. He didn't know the names of the songs or the artists. He hadn't done this since college. He fit one in and cued it up, forwarding the leader to the red mark.

A screech interrupted the white noise, and he pressed that earpiece against his head. A blip, then nothing.

"Come on," Jorge said, impatient, when any number of things could have happened to Rafael.

The reggae faded, and Jorge opened the mike.

"A little technical difficulty there," he apologized, trying to mimic the jazzy, false style of the host. He could do a good Vin Scully from *The Game of the Week,* even a decent Joe Garagiola. "We'll try and take care of things here. In the meantime, here's Alicia Camacho with 'Too Much Love.'"

It was a samba he didn't recognize. The other earpiece was just fuzz.

Gloria and Felipe came running past the window and in. When he took the headphones off, he could hear the rattle of small arms—close, maybe a block away.

"They're downstairs," Gloria said, breathing hard. "I don't know how they got here so fast."

"From the armory," Felipe said.

Jorge couldn't think. "Find a window on that side. I want to know what's going on."

"We did." Felipe pointed across the hall. "It's at least a platoon."

Outside, a heavy machine gun let loose; a siren wound up, announcing an air raid. It was all turning to shit on him, and he couldn't think. They wanted an answer.

"Do what you can," Jorge said, and fit the headphones on again.

Still nothing. They were six minutes into the landing.

He thought of just telling the people it was a success, to arm themselves and come out and help. But what if it wasn't, what if it turned into a massacre? How many years had these people been waiting? How many more before they'd get another chance?

How the earth moves when we are one, Alicia Camacho crooned over a steel band. *How I die each time, how I die, how I die.*

Nothing.

He lifted the earpiece free and heard the screaming of MiGs, then blocked it out again, found another song and cued it up in the second cassette. The coda faded away.

"All right. Sounds a little dangerous outside right now," he told Santa Rosa. "We'll have news coming up in just a few, so stay with us."

He hit play and made sure it ran, then took off the one set of headphones and concentrated on the static.

"Come on," he said.

As if in answer, a voice broke through, the transmission stretching and compressing it, making it waver, high and munchkinlike.

"Ortega," it squeaked, helium-funny.

Jorge hit the interrupt button and stopped the song.

"I copy," he said, amused by Rafael's voice, giddy that the whole thing might actually work. Outside, the streets were full of automatic fire. It was ridiculous, it was nuts.

"Ortega," he repeated, as Jorge had taught him. His voice was deep now, mellow, all over the place, as if it were being scrambled. Jorge pressed the headphones tight against his ears so he could hear better.

"*Sí,* I copy."

"This is Lieutenant Victor Clemente of the People's Army of Cuba."

Jorge let go of the headphones and sat there staring at the spilled coffee, sure he'd heard him wrong.

"Ortega," Clemente said. "You're surrounded. Surrender or die."

CHAPTER 28

HE FOUND THEM IN an office across the hall, firing from the windows—foolishly, their barrels sticking out so the muzzle flashes gave them away. The lack of training angered him. It was just his frustration with Clemente, he understood, and what he imagined they'd done to Rafael to make him confess everything.

To the south, the ballpark's light towers ruled the skyline.

He tapped Felipe on the back. "We've got to go," he shouted.

Below, a bus was on fire in the middle of the street, and he could see the *guardia* using the smoke to maneuver. One of them disappeared beneath the marquee.

"What happened?" Gloria asked.

"I don't know," Jorge said. "Rafael's not coming through."

He rigged the plastique for ten minutes and they ran down the hall. The elevator was waiting for them. He pressed 1. Though it was probably too late to save them, he had to try. Even as he punched the button, he knew it wasn't a good command decision. Did he want to be a martyr? Maybe it was blood—his father had turned himself into one.

"What about our famous retreat?" Felipe asked.

"They're still down there," Gloria argued, and Jorge wondered if she knew the odds. It didn't matter; she was with him on this.

"It's selfish." Felipe leaned past him and hit 2. "I won't let them get you. The rest of us, fine, we're nothing. But not you."

Jorge ignored him, watching the numbers. Gloria found his hand and linked their fingers.

"You can't," the old man said, taking him by the shoulders. "We need you too much."

"And let them die?" Gloria asked.

"They're prepared. We should stick with the plan."

"You're afraid," she accused him.

"I'm *thinking* because no one else is!"

As they dropped, the firing became plain, the chattering of AKs, glass shattering. He caught an acrid whiff of tear gas.

The elevator settled on 2. The doors opened but none of them moved.

"*Tonto!*" Felipe said, and hit the door open button. "You are Cuba. You can't die yet." He lifted his AK to Jorge's face, his own filled with helplessness, and while Jorge didn't like it, he knew the old man was right. They were probably already dead.

He looked to Gloria and saw that it was his decision.

Felipe waited.

"You'll come too," Jorge made sure.

"Yes," the old man said, "but now. *Vámonos!*"

Jorge frowned, letting him know he didn't approve, then spun out into the hallway, leading with his sixteen.

It was clear, and he waved Gloria on. She hustled past and dropped to one knee, crouched against the wall. Jorge looked back to signal Felipe and saw the doors closing, the old man standing there with his AK across his chest.

"*Viva Cuba Libre!*" Felipe shouted, a fist in the air.

Jorge lunged for the doors, but they touched and the number went dark.

The cable sang and the 1 lit up. They heard the doors slide open and a ripping burst from Felipe's AK—drowned by a wave of automatic fire.

Jorge banged his fist against the doors. "Stupid old *cabrón.*"

The cable hummed.

"Come on!" Gloria called, and they ran for the back stairwell.

He led her down to the sub-basement, where the heating system rumbled and the lights were protected by metal cages. The place was a maze. Felipe had told him where to go. There was a freight elevator that surfaced in a back alley. If they could make it to the parking garage across the street, they could go down another block and have a good shot at the *mercado* and then the ballpark. It was too early for the chopper Forbes had promised, but they could hole up at the stadium and wait. As they raced down the dim corridors, he lied to himself about their chances. Nothing had gone right so far; why should that change now?

Behind them, shouts, footsteps ringing down stairwells. The fighting nattered above, distant, inconsequential. They sprinted past locked cages filled with office furniture, pallets of toilet paper. It was tempting to think they could find a place to hide and come out sometime next week, but he knew Clemente wouldn't let him get away. They'd show his bloodless body on TV as a warning, like the professor's, like Catalina's.

They reached a dead end, a wall of dusty file cabinets and presswood desks, dirty mail carts stacked inside one another like Dixie cups.

"Are you sure it's here?" Gloria asked, gasping.

"The *viejo* said so."

"Then where is it?"

They were stopped, squabbling, when an enormous noise made the earth shake, Gloria stumbling back into him. A lightbulb popped in its cage, the glass sprinkling down. It confused Jorge; it was too big for the plastique.

"Mother of God," Gloria said, and crossed herself. Before she was finished, a smaller blast made them duck—the plastique.

Another huge one knocked dust from the ceiling.

"Bombs," Jorge guessed.

"So the attack is real."

"I think so."

"*Viva* America!"

"Not yet," Jorge warned.

They retraced their way through the maze, jogging back toward the calls of the *guardia*, the echoing footsteps. They pushed through the first set of unexplored doors into a concrete-block hall. A second set was paneled with dented steel, as if it had been rammed. Inside, a forklift stood at the top of a long ramp, and there beside it stood the freight elevator.

It was just a platform with a scratched steel arch to push open the doors in the ceiling. A greased track ran up one wall. The controls were on a post—red for up, black for down. Jorge pressed the button and with a jolt they rose. They stood back to back, ready, their weapons leveled.

The arch banged against the doors and separated them, letting in the sun, the sound of nearby gunfire, sirens. The doors opened slowly, parted like a drawbridge. Jorge was facing a brick wall, and he turned to help Gloria cover a parking lot, rows of cars on fire, the smoke from their tires thick—perfect cover.

He expected the *guardia* to be there, a tank, a Saracen, but there was no one, only civilians wandering around dazed, some bleeding, wailing, holding their hands to their foreheads. Down the alley rose a pyramid of rubble, the brick dust still lifting from it. A few blocks over, a column of smoke mushroomed. The air was filled with Werewolves.

They sent the platform down again and jumped off. Gloria swaddled her AK in her shawl. He made sure he had his pistol and pitched his sixteen into the weeds. No one paid them any attention. A mother stumbled past with a squalling infant, bleeding from the ears; the man following her wore a sport coat but no pants, a chunk of his knee missing. Gloria clutched Jorge's arm, the AK hard between them. She was crying—from relief or pity, it didn't matter. Jorge circled her with his arms and kept walking, the smoke bringing tears to his eyes. They blended in with the civilians, huddled like refugees, headed for the safety of the parking garage.

But at the corner Gloria turned for the front of the station, breaking away from him. Jorge caught her by the arm, the shawl pulling back to show the AK's muzzle.

"I have to see," she said, her eyes wild, and he thought of them all dead, laid out like El Marichal's band.

146

"You don't want to."

"I have to see," she repeated flatly, in control, and he thought of Catalina, how he'd needed to see what the Operator had done to her. It was not guilt precisely. That came later. At the time he'd considered it merely his duty to her, his first payment for what he'd done. He'd found the truck with just one hundred dollars in bribes. He wanted to apologize, to say to her face that he hadn't meant for this to happen. In the end he'd turned away, stumbled along the muddy, rutted road, already trying to wipe the picture of what lay under the tarp from his mind. Now he wished he'd stayed and honored his responsibility, taken a long, hard look. Instead, he'd run away. Since then he'd been nothing—until now.

Gloria's eyes were defiant. The firing had quieted.

"All right," he said, afraid it was a mistake. Hell, he thought; the park would be quicker anyway.

THE BUS LAY CHARRED on its side, the seats and window moldings still flickering. The marquee was riddled with holes, the tinted windows gone, scattered across the sidewalk. A squad of *guardia* in rubber gloves were hauling the bodies out, tossing them into an army truck. Glass snapped and crunched under their boots. Jorge recognized the two guards by their uniforms. The truck was running, as if someone wanted the bodies, and with an incredible, hateful pleasure Jorge thought Clemente would be disappointed.

A pair of soldiers brought out Hector and swung him up into the bed, his head banging the tailgate. He was still wearing his do-rag, his face a boy's.

"Murderers," Gloria said blankly. "Bastards."

Jorge squeezed her hand, but she didn't seem to notice, transfixed by the destruction.

"God will punish them," she said to no one. She was shaking, her face clenched, and he stroked her shoulder.

Another pair had Francisco by the wrists and ankles, part of his face shot away; his cowboy hat was missing, revealing a bald spot. It took three of them to heft César up, rolling him off their shoulders.

Luz was burned, naked to the waist. It was his fault, he thought, and he was glad he'd seen them, to understand what he'd done. He should-n't have left them downstairs, he should have told the old man to go to hell in that elevator, ridden it down with him.

Close by, someone opened up with an AK, and Jorge ducked, instinctively reaching for his pistol.

It was Gloria, beside him, raking the station with fire. She had the AK at her hip, swiveling, gritting her teeth. A spray of blood flew from one of the soldiers carrying Felipe. The other dropped jerking to the sidewalk, Felipe rolling over his legs as if tackling him. Gloria hosed down the windows, glass tinkling, sparks jumping from the marble.

Jorge swore and swung around, covering her back with his pistol. A soldier bolted from behind the bus and Jorge emptied a clip at him, finally bringing him down. He popped another in and swore at the pistol—it wasn't enough gun for this shit. He dove behind the truck and peeked between the tires. Gloria was still blazing away. It would have been nice, he thought, if she'd told him.

The exhaust was hot on his face, and he remembered the truck was running. He got up and ran for her, waving the pistol like a TV cop. He reached her just as she finished her clip. She stood there spent, finished, as if they could kill her now.

"Arriba," he called, and grabbed her arm, and they ran for the truck.

They piled through the driver's-side door, Jorge pushing her into the other seat. Outside, the *guardia* were returning fire, rounds whip-ping through the canvas, thumping into the rear. He found first and popped the clutch, swung the truck past the rear of the bus and into the wide open street. The truck was slow, the engine burning, and then he remembered the emergency brake. They roared through a blinking yellow, headed downtown.

"What the fuck are you doing?" he yelled at her.

"I killed them. That's what we're supposed to do."

"It was stupid."

"I don't care!" she screamed.

A Saracen turned onto the street ahead of them, its turret point-ed the wrong way, and Jorge braked and cut the truck left, headed for the *mercado*. The tank in the parking garage was somewhere around here. He stayed in the middle lane, weaving between abandoned cars, keeping his speed up, hoping to blow by it. They were only a few blocks away; he could already see the ocean sky, dotted with Werewolves and maybe even some of their own choppers. If they were bombing, he thought, it was serious. It was real.

Something banged against the roof, and his thigh stung. He was bleeding. They both looked up and there was a hole in the ceiling.

"Sniper!" Gloria cried, grabbing her AK.

He swerved, making them a harder target. The blood welled out over his chinos. He could feel his foot going numb.

"Can you drive?" she asked, fumbling with a clip.

"I don't know."

"I can't," she said. "I never learned."

It made him laugh, he didn't know why. She was funny.

Another bang, and she grunted as if punched. The AK fell into the footwell.

"You okay?"

He looked over. She regarded him sleepily, drunk, and then her eyes rolled back and she pitched forward against the dash, the back of her head a mess, her hair sticky.

He stood on the brakes and the truck coughed and stalled.

Her eyes were fixed, her shoulder soaking. She wasn't breathing, but he leaned his ear down to her mouth anyway.

The roof banged, and a round drilled a jagged hole in the dash, paint chips pricking his face.

"Gloria," he pleaded, and he thought of Miami and her new teeth, his apartment, the mornings eating cereal on the balcony. They weren't lies; if they lived, he would have made good on all of his promises. It didn't matter that the odds had never been with them.

He laid his cheek against her chest and smelled her skin one last time. The sirens whined, rising again. He had to go, he had to leave her, but not the same way he'd abandoned Catalina. This was different.

A round slammed through the hood, releasing a puff of steam.

Jorge swore at the man for interrupting him.

He plucked a strand of hair free of her lashes. Her head was wet on his shoulder. It was love; she'd brought him back to the living, made him capable again. He told her so and kissed her, closing his eyes, feeling her teeth so he'd remember what she'd given him. This time he didn't think of anyone else at all.

CHAPTER

HE CONVINCED THE TRUCK to start again and nursed it down the street and around a corner, out of range. His leg was rubbery, and shifting was a problem. The engine lurched and failed, spurted as if he'd run out of gas. Steam poured from the hood, misting the windshield. He leaned over the wheel to avoid cars parked in the middle of intersections.

The sidewalks were empty and oddly quiet, occasionally someone running from one doorway to another, but no troops, no bodies, no house-to-house fighting. The tank had left the parking garage, the curb crushed where the treads had rolled over it. Maybe Clemente had contained everything down by the harbor, Jorge thought. But the bombardment. Part of the diversion—a quick strike by a few F-111s, not more than two or three sorties. It fit with the rest of the evidence. Then it was just as well they'd failed.

He kept it in second, the clutch useless. His leg burned where he'd been hit, and he wondered if it had gotten the bone. On the floor, his blood mixed with Gloria's. She lay against the door, jiggling with the bumps, her hair over her face. The truck shuddered, the engine clacking. By the time he passed the vacant *mercado,* he couldn't feel his toes.

The ballpark was untouched, its light towers rising into blue sky. The truck coughed across the lot. Jorge let it stall behind the grandstand and checked his watch. He was right on time.

He fell getting out, his pistol clattering on the blacktop. The asphalt was hot, and he raised himself up on the truck's running board, the open door. The pain made him nauseous, off-balance, the lined grid of parking spots tilting. Gloria slumped across the seat, her mouth open as if she were sleeping. Jorge closed the door and limped toward the entrance, dragging his dead leg along with both hands.

Above, there were nothing but Werewolves, a rare old MiG screaming across the harbor. The bombing had stopped. He remembered the fallen building downtown. The jets were too accurate for that. It must have been a naval barrage, launched far offshore. He couldn't figure out what that meant, whether they were serious or not. He strained to hear the crackle of small arms, but there was nothing. No one had landed. So it was a diversion, he'd suspected it all along. They'd tried something up north, he hoped. The question was, would Forbes send someone to get him? Jorge thought he deserved at least that. He'd kept his part of the bargain.

The stadium gates were open, the turnstiles deserted. Old gum dotted the concrete. Below, the field shone a brilliant green, barbered and crosshatched, the walls beyond the warning track plastered with advertisements. He made his way down to the home team's dugout, leaning a stiff arm on the aisle seats, swinging the dead leg like a crutch. It took far too long; if there was a sniper there, he was dead. His boot was full of blood; it squished with every step.

He reached the railing separating the fans from the field and swung himself over, falling again, hard, the fine dirt powdering his cheeks, peppering his hair. He made sure he had the pistol and dragged himself up and across the neatly trimmed grass, grunting, to the pitcher's mound. He sat down on the rubber, facing the outfield, and arranged his leg.

"All right," he said. "Come get me."

The blood was still pulsing, soaking his chinos, but he was not strong enough to get a tourniquet on it. He felt drunk, breathless, his head loose on his neck, his eyes going all over the place, like at the end of a wild night.

He clicked the clip out to make sure it was full. It took him three tries to jam it in again. Since his father's death he'd sworn he would never kill himself. This was no different. He'd take as many of them with him as he could. His father had not had that choice, he supposed.

He took *me*, Jorge thought.

The TV was still on when the cops brought him in. The Rangers were beating the Angels. His father was laid out in the chair, slumped down as if he were sleeping, the gun a few feet away. He'd left a note on the tray table with all of the other papers. *I love you*, it said. Jorge scoffed at first, bitterly, and then he saw it was addressed not to him but to his mother. His father begged her forgiveness, not his, as if he didn't need it. Now Jorge wondered if it made any difference. Probably not. After Catalina, he'd stopped believing in the possibility of forgiveness. He didn't want to be absolved. After Gloria, was it still true?

No, in just these three days he'd changed. He'd given his best, everything he had—like a tiring reliever going to his money pitch—and if it wasn't enough, he had at least tried. There was some honor in that. Even now, knowing Forbes wasn't coming, he was thankful for the chance, as if he'd fulfilled his destiny. It was a relief, a blessing even.

He checked his watch and then the sky. He needed to rest, to sleep. It was shock, he thought; he was losing too much blood. The empty seats attended him, and the press box, expectant.

"The great Ortega," he said. Now he knew how his grandfather had felt that last day—all of Cuba betrayed, forgotten, lost.

He remembered Catalina, how her last minutes must have been. It was his fault, though he couldn't have known how far they'd go. If he had been a man, he would have killed himself then. Instead he'd waited. And had this redeemed him? Part of him wanted to think so, but no. He was still his father's son. You couldn't run from it; it was the blood.

All Saturday afternoon they watched TV, the network double-header. When his father finished his beer he gave Jorge the can and he ran upstairs to get him a cold one.

"Thanks, sport," his father said, and cracked it and gave him a bitter, bubbly sip.

A fluttering reached him, and dizzily he looked up to the sun. A squadron of Werewolves heeled off, came over the stadium, making for Arriaga and the north. As he watched a second diamond fly over, he lost his balance and fell back against the mound. He couldn't lift himself up. So it was over. Too bad.

He thought he heard cheering, far-off applause, or was it just the rush of turbines, the waves on shore? At home the fans cheered for you even when you were losing. That's what it meant to be a fan, that belief that eventually justice would be done, the good rewarded and the evil punished. It might take a lifetime—generations even—but one day, if you had faith, your team would be victorious. There was heartbreak, yes, but you suffered, you waited, you didn't give up. You believed.

Viva Cuba, Felipe said. Good for him, the old *cabrón*.

Jorge tried to say it, but his tongue was stuck. It came out a growl.

He rolled over on his side, the gun caught beneath him. He wanted it now but his arm wouldn't respond. He couldn't feel his finger on the trigger. It was not just shock. Fine, he'd expected it.

The sun was hot on him and he wanted to vomit, and then that passed and he swallowed hard and suddenly he was freezing. He closed his eyes and opened them again. The heat made waves over the outfield grass. The sky was a wall, one unblemished color. A pennant flapped on top of the scoreboard, the wind blowing in. It was an old manual scoreboard, deep green, with a box for every half inning. The slot for the visiting team was empty. It was a shame, Jorge thought, gazing at the barren stands. Even his father would agree: it was a perfect day for a game.